A JOURNEY OF LOVE

STARSEEDS

SUE PATERSON

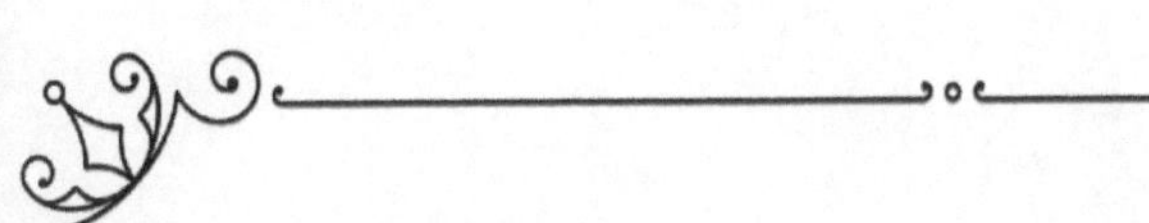

DEDICATION

To the Paqos, Porters and
Guides of Peru...
Your footsteps echo with
wisdom, strength and inspiration

PROLOGUE

September 1999

"It was like watching God die… I've never felt so humbled. In his last breaths, he was watching over me." The old farmer pulled a ratty handkerchief out of his pocket.

"Exquisite pain," his wife said. "More than a human heart can understand."

"Twenty-six… old for a llama, yet he chose his time. Equinox called him. So many endings in the fall." The old farmer buried his face in his hands. "My heart is broken."

"I watched you from the window," she said. "Moonlight in your hair as you stretched out on the ground next to him, you a tiny human next to a four-hundred-pound llama, the gentleness in your movement as you covered him with the blanket."

"I'll never go into a grocery store again without asking myself if we need apples or carrots for the llamas. Won't be the same, getting up in the morning and looking out and not seeing Bacardi there. When Domingo left us, we managed. But now…"

"Good for guarding livestock we were told, but did ya notice each night the llamas positioned themselves in front of the barn door? It was us they protected. Our home." She chuckled, reaching down to tousle her husband's curly grey hair. "All these years, living in a barn, just footsteps separating us from the llamas and chickens. Divine protection… whatever did we do to deserve them?"

"Someone's looking out for us." He shrugged. "As daylight broke, that deer came by. You know, the one who used to come in the mornings?"

"She'd jump the fence and sit with Bacardi as the chickens and ducks ran around. Once she even brought her fawn."

"I lost track of time, but earlier in the night, the owl perched in the tree over the creek, hooting - came to say goodbye. It's sacred ground we live on. Llamas have always known that... have been part of the sacred forever."

ONE

April 1977

Daylight crept in, casting sunbeams through the clouds that shrouded the mountains encircling the Incan Lost City of Light. High on an upper terrace of Machu Picchu, a white llama stood, his alabaster form emerging as the fog lifted and dissolved into dawn. Across a deep gorge, he greeted Little Sister Mountain Putucusi, her trees shimmering as the morning breeze cleared the clouds, revealing patches of blue sky. The breath of the wind carried her laughter, a song as old as the earth itself. King Llama's gaze wandered to the distant mountaintops, where ancestors ascended upon completing their earth journey, now guardians whose spirits were woven into the fabric of time. His reign stretched across many human lifetimes, his soul a keeper of wisdom. Soon he would join the ancestors, but not today. His ears perked, and his heart filled with the news that two magical beings were soon to be born into the world.

And indeed, in the wee hours of morning, two seedpods spiraled down from the highest star, landing at his feet with a shimmer like fallen moonlight. King Llama bowed his head, for he knew these special beings cradled the essence of magic, wisdom and healing. Churning the sacred medicine in his three stomachs, little by little, infusing the seedpods with the breath of the mountains and the wisdom of the ages, he shaped them with his tongue until they grew - not very big, just big enough to carry the weight of destiny. Then, the moment came. With a knowing glint in his ancient eyes and a final swish of his tongue, King Llama tilted his long neck back, braced his powerful stance and spat, perhaps the greatest spit of all time, launching the Star Seeds like magic bullets to the north.

Shimmering with a green glow, the Starseeds sped through the universe, laughing in glee as they ricocheted off mountains, dipped into rivers, and soared north through stars, rain, and sunshine. Mother Moon, flushed with delight, stepped out of their way. Reports of shooting stars and flying objects made headlines, and people watched from backyards and roadsides to see these bright flashes of light as they sped through the sky, unaware they were seeing the return of the ancient, the divine.

After swirling through time and space for many moons, gathering wisdom from oceans, seas, mountains, and deserts – after stopping to kiss the sun and hug the moon, the Star Seeds hovered over a large, rolling meadow. Circling, they waited for just the right moment, and as the sun rose, spiraled like a funnel and tumbled into the tall grass, surprised to discover they had long wobbly legs and spindly necks. Blinking in wonder, they felt the earth's heartbeat under their hooves and the breath of the wind against their soft, downy coats. Above them, they watched as the green light that carried them spun into a ball and sped off into the heavens.

King Llama watched their luminous ascent, a shadow of concern crossing his heart. He knew the world was desperate for the healing and wisdom only a llama could bring. But would these young ones remember their purpose? Would they hear the call of the mountains? His spirit, so long bound to the earth, trembled with the weight of uncertainty. Worried about becoming forgetful in his older years, he turned to the ever-knowing presence of Little Sister Mountain Putucusi, seeking her counsel.

Opening her arms, she stroked the long, thick coat of her old friend with the breeze, and together they sat under the silver gaze of the moon and joined their minds, sending love and guidance to the young ones, speeding through space and time. While the journey ahead would be long, stars never lost their way, and neither would those who carried their light.

King Llama, sighing in relief, smiled at Little Sister Mountain Putucusi. Together, they closed their eyes, feeling the lineage take form, sensing the ancient wisdom of the llama nation coursing once more through newborn veins. The all-seeing eyes of their kind had returned to the world. The balance was kept. The journey had begun.

TWO

The old farmer in Northern Oregon pulled on his overalls and buttoned the straps. Somehow, he knew it was going to be a special day. Bones creaking in time with the floorboards of the old house, he tip-toed through the bedroom, heading to the kitchen to get the coffee started. Pausing, he looked down at Liza, his wife, long wisps of gray curls falling over the edge of the pillow as she stirred.

"There's a hole in the bucket, dear Henry, dear Henry. There's a hole in the bucket, dear Henry, a hole," she whispered, eyes closed.

"You're dreaming, dear Liza, dear Liza, you see? You're dreaming, dear Liza…" *Now I'm doing it.* Chuckling, he pulled the doorknob closed and snuck into the kitchen, wanting to drink his coffee in peace before she got up and handed him the familiar honey-do list. Percolator plugged in, he looked out the window as the coffee danced and made its glug-glug sounds. He knew there was a hole in the bucket, but today there was magic in the air. Pouring the coffee into his tall, red mug that said "DAD," he watched the liquid as it steamed, marveling at the new technology. The coffee pot had been a gift from his boys. In these quiet moments in the morning, he could still see them, dressed in matching pajamas, excitement in their adolescent eyes as he unwrapped the gift and pulled out the coffee maker. "Percolator… what in the world?" Giggling, they handed him his second gift, the cup that said: DAD. Tears welled in his eyes as he took the first sip, feeling the energy of his people, his lineage woven into this land across generations. A pang of loneliness settled in his stomach as he wondered if he and Liza were the last of the line.

He walked over and looked out the window, pondering what was different about this day. "Something…" he mumbled, running his fingers through his wavy gray hair as he watched the sun reach over the treetops and pour into the kitchen, slipping past the yellow-gingham curtains to dance checkered patterns on the wall.

The llamas ran through the grass, unable to restrain the joy of being free. Knees buckling, they fell over and over, laughing at each other. Startled at the sounds of gurgling and grumbling from their three tiny stomachs, they stopped and looked at each other in curiosity. There must be more they should know.

The black llama knelt on the ground, slowly lowering his hind end. *The answer must be here,* he thought, putting his nose in the grass and rubbing it all around. Filled with the scent of the grass, he lay on his side, absorbing energy from the earth. He had been sure the answer would be there but was puzzled at the empty feeling still coming from his rumbling stomachs. The white llama stood nearby and gave his brother a funny look that said: "You silly llama. You're supposed to eat the grass, not roll around in it." The white llama munched and munched, feeling his first stomach fill, then his second and as he was working on the third, he saw the black llama stand, watching him with unblinking eyes, big as saucers.

The black llama put his nose back into the grass, letting it tickle his face, and then closing his eyes, took a nibble. The sweetness of it made his mouth water and his heart sing. The earth had given him the answer after all. Bellies full, the sun warm on their new bodies and cradled by the soft downy grass, they closed their eyes for a moment, chewing their cud. Drifting into a dream, they felt a smile stretch across the universe from King Llama, high atop Machu Picchu.

Henry pulled his straw hat off the hook by the back door and turned the handle just as Liza came into the kitchen. "Coffee's on," he said, stepping out of the door.

"But Henry…" she called.

"I know… there's a hole in the bucket," he mumbled under his breath. Climbing up onto the old tractor, excitement filled him as the engine roared to life. A smile tugged at the corner of his mouth at the grind of the gears as he shoved it into first and headed out to the pasture. It had been a while since he rode the width and breadth of his land. Driving through the shade of the old willows, nostalgia filled him at the sight of the old wooden swing hanging from the branches. He could almost hear the laughter of his boys, legs pumping to go higher.

"More, more," they would yell, begging for another push.

Seems like yesterday…

Sighing, he continued driving along the creek. Happy little whispers of sunlight shone through the trees, and ripples of water danced over rocks as the water rushed by.

Creeks high, he thought, reminded of last winter's endless drenching rain.

The tractor lurched as it hit an overgrown tree root, sending a jolt of pain from Henry's back down to his foot. Grimacing, he rubbed out the ache in his leg and let the tractor idle for a moment, gazing out over the land he'd tended for so many years. His heart filled with gratitude for all the gifts he'd been given. Patting the steering wheel, he said: "Harvester, at the end of the day, it was all worth it. You've been good to me."

Turning, he headed towards the trees that marked the natural boundary of his property. Looking down at the fuel gauge, he felt a wave of relief to see the little red arrow at the halfway mark. It used to be that he could run out of gas, jump off the tractor, jog to the barn, grab a can of gas and jog back. But not anymore. Following the fence line, he spotted two shapes sitting in the grass near the trees in the distance. Didn't quite look like deer.

What the heck?

On the top of Machu Picchu, King Llama stood in solemn watch over the sacred terraces below. His ageless eyes, pools of untold wisdom, followed the birds as they glided effortlessly over the stone city, perching upon treetops and roofs, weaving their morning songs in the crisp mountain air. The mist unraveled like a whispered secret, revealing the winding Inca trail far below, bringing the first visitors of the morning to the sacred site. Soon, the ancient pathways would be full of people, drawn by an unseen force, yearning for wisdom, for healing. But for now, they were tiny specks on the ground, moving like ants.

King Llama sighed at the years of absorbing the energy from the broken hearts, aching bodies and wounded souls. Travelers were unaware that they would have burdens lifted and absorbed by the llama nation by taking this journey. And young ones, such as the newly born star seeds, didn't even know yet that a llama brought healing to the world. Just by being.

He recalled a child from long ago, one of the rare ones, an old soul in a young body. This boy had met his gaze and held it, unafraid, untouched by doubt. In that fleeting moment, recognition passed between them, a promise written in the language of the stars. They had stood gazing into each other's eyes for several moments before the little boy's mother whisked him away from "that dangerous animal." King Llama chuckled to himself at the memory. Dangerous indeed. That child would one day become a great healer, carrying the seed of knowing deep within him, waiting for the right moment to awaken.

The breeze picked up and King Llama lifted his head toward the sky, nostrils flaring, sensing renewed life. In that Oregon pasture, where ancient roots met new soil, the star seeds were stirring. A great awakening was happening. And the mountains listened.

Liza poured the hot, steaming coffee into the mug that said: MOM. She opened the refrigerator and took out a carton of milk, longing for the days when they had fresh cream from their own cows. But things had changed, and they could no longer manage as they had in the old days. Henry and Liza had prayed for someone to carry on the farm and keep the lineage alive, but it didn't seem that was going to happen.

A far way look had been in Henry's eyes this morning as he snuck past the bed. He didn't think she noticed, but she had. A woman of faith, Liza knew prayers were always answered. Yet, she also knew that answers often came in unexpected ways and long after one had forgotten that they had even prayed for it. The heaviness of what felt like an unanswered prayer lay in her heart.

The carton of cream was cold as she absentmindedly poured it into her coffee, flinching as the hot liquid overflowed. "Oh, Liza," she murmured, "what's to become of you?" Bending down, she slurped some off the top, then grabbed a towel to wipe up the mess.

Mindful of the ache in her fingers as the refrigerator door latch snapped shut, she turned to the sound of the tractor roaring to life. Sipping her coffee, Liza stood at the window and watched Henry's back as he rode out onto their land, smiling as he passed the buckets by the side of the barn. In the old days they would tease each other, singing as the boys got ready for school:

*"There's a hole in the bucket, dear Liza, dear Liza.
There's a hole in the bucket, dear Liza a hole."*

She could hear the kids giggle at their silliness and smiled, humming the old traditional rhyme:

*"So fix it dear Henry, dear Henry, dear Henry.
So fix it dear Henry, dear Henry, fix it."*

Later, as teenagers, they just rolled their eyes. But it had kept her and Henry young and even a little feisty. Occasionally, as they watched the school bus drive away from the end of the gravel driveway, with raised eyebrows and a twinkle of invitation in his eyes, he would take her hand and lead her into the barn. Kisses and giggles later, the chores would wait as they lingered over an extra cup of coffee. But that was then. She wondered what would become of them now.

THREE

Against the tall pines, on the highest point of the land, the llamas, black and white mirrors of each other, sat like bookends, chewing their cud. Heads held high, their ears perked up like antennas at the sound of the tractor. Knowledge and wisdom flowed through their veins, reminding them that they knew that this sound would come at some point in time. Curious about everything, they wondered what it was, as much as they wondered about anything. Turning their long necks, they looked at each other. With a nod of acknowledgment, they continued sitting, regal like princes, waiting patiently as the tractor came into view. The old farmer bounced on the seat as the tractor rolled up the hill towards them.

Always alert for danger, no small detail went unnoticed by the llamas. But on this day, a quiet feeling told them this might be a friend. But how could one be sure? Bending at their knees and raising their hind ends, they stood, legs still wobbly. Five thousand miles away, on Machu Picchu, King Llama looked up from his grazing and smiled at Little Sister Mountain Putucusi, who squeezed her arms together as if sending him a hug.

Henry's heart beat a little faster as the tractor chugged up the hill, squinting at the two animals. *Llamas? How could that be? And young ones...*

But last Sunday at church, he'd overheard talk about a farmer in the next town over getting llamas.

" Good for predator control," the man said. "And easy to take care of."

But where in the world did these two come from? It's like they sprang up out of thin air!

Seeing the llamas stand, Henry let the tractor roll to a stop and turned it off. For the first time in his years as a farmer, he didn't know what to do.

Don't want to scare them… and certainly can't outrun 'em… maybe I should go and get Liza. She could always gentle the young, scared calves…

The llamas stared at him with curious brown eyes, ears flickering as if they, too, were a little confused about how to proceed. Henry pulled his straw hat, which had fallen onto his shoulders, back on his head, then edged his butt across the seat, planting his foot firmly on the step. Swinging his other foot over, he felt the old catch in his hip but was able to shake it out before jumping down on the ground. *Getting' old, Henry.*

Henry walked towards the llamas, but stopped as he saw them stretch their necks even longer and bend their ears back. Moving slowly, he took another step, holding his hands in plain sight, but the closer he got, the more their ears flattened against their heads. He didn't know much about llamas, but he knew enough to recognize when to stop, and that they spit.

Gotta get Liza… He backed away but stopped as his foot landed on the tractor's first step. Years of tending cattle had taught him to stand his ground and not give up. Turning around, he pulled a handful of grass from the ground, leaned against the rear tire and pulled his hat down over his eyes: He stuck a piece of grass in his mouth and whispered: "Gimme the best you got."

⭐

King Llama knelt upon the earth. Deep in meditation, he let the mountain's ancient pulse steady his soul. His message to the world had always been: "All will be well." It was a truth woven into the fabric of existence, yet even he, the guardian of wisdom, felt a fleeting whisper of doubt from time to time. Lifting his gaze, he turned to Little Sister Mountain Putucusi.

"It's not always a smooth ride, even for the magical ones," she murmured, her voice carried on the wind like a gentle song. "Little by little, they'll learn friend from foe, know when to trust and when not. It'll take time and experience."

A breeze came up and the mountain shivered in knowing as the leaves on her trees rustled, shimmering in the afternoon light. The road was never easy, not even for the luminous ones. But the stars still guided, the earth still listened, and the journey, however winding, always led home.

The black llama looked at the white llama. "Now what?" he asked with a flicker of his ears. The white llama stood back and watched while his brother took one tentative step forward and then another. As he reached the big wheel of the tractor, he looked back but saw his brother hadn't budged. Uncertain of the best move, he stood staring at the farmer, sniffing the air around him, but curiosity got the best of him, and he leaned in. Standing still, Henry let his hand with the bunch of grass in it loosen and continued to chew on the grass sticking out of his mouth, pretending to ignore the animal.

The black llama sniffed the tire, then reached down and nuzzled the grass in Henry's hand. The sensation of the soft lips tickled a little and Henry felt a giggle rise in his belly, chuckling under his breath. At the sound, the llama nudged Henry's hand, then sniffed up his arm and nibbling the grass hanging out of his mouth, knocked Henry's hat off.

"Whoa, boy," Henry pulled back slightly, but the llama, now intrigued, pushed his nose into Henry's gray curls. Henry put his arm up and tried to duck away, but with little room to move, hit his head on the edge of the seat. "God darn it, stop!"

The llama backed away, ears flattened against his head and mouth raised, ready to spit. But he had never spit before, and even though he felt like his top stomach was going to erupt, he was a little confused. Henry ducked his face behind his arm, bracing for the worst, but when he peeked out under the crease of his elbow, the llama had turned and ran back to his brother.

As Henry drove away, he put his hand over his chest. "Heart attack? No, don't think so." He took the handkerchief from his pocket and wiped the sweat from his brow. "Stroke? Nope, not that." Reaching the edge of the field, he let the tractor come to a stop, turned around, and looked behind him. The llamas were staring at him as he drove away. "Yep, that really happened."

The llamas watched the tractor fade out of sight. The more cautious of the two, the white llama flattened his ears and made a low humming sound to show his displeasure with the black llama's reckless behavior. But being young, he soon forgot his anger and returned to grazing on the long, green grass, making his way along the stretch of pines to a trail that led to the creek. The black llama, miffed, as he thought he had been very brave, followed at a distance. His black bushy tail disappeared between the trees as he followed his brother over the rough ground towards the water. They stood looking at ripples dancing across the rocks and glanced at each other out of the corner of their eye, wondering what to do next. Water splashed up from the nearest boulder, hitting them in the face. The white llama jerked his head back, then stuck his long tongue out and licked the water off his nose. Surprised at how good it felt in his mouth, he put his nose down into the water, sucking in a whole bunch. But it didn't go anywhere and ran out of his mouth and back into the creek. Puzzled, he took in another big gulp and, this time, raised his nose to the sky. As the water trickled down, he marveled at the sensation on the back of his throat, making a little gurgle in his first stomach. He looked over at his brother triumphantly. The black llama stuck the tip of his nose into the water, then with a mouth full, tilted his head up, enjoying the coolness of this new sensation.

Liza smoothed the pale blue chenille bedspread into place and fluffed the pillows. Peeking into the laundry bin, she found only a few items and closed the lid. Headed to the kitchen, she paused by her dressing table and picked up a tortoiseshell hairbrush from the mirrored tray. Brushing her hair had always felt good and today was no exception. Setting it down, she traced the wrinkles on her face, then touched a tube of cherry red lipstick. For a second, she thought about putting some on, but jumped at the shrill sound of the phone ringing. Hurrying to the kitchen, she grabbed the yellow wall phone.

"Oh, hello, Helen."

The door opened and Henry walked in, eyes excited.

"Liza…"

"Helen, can I call you back?" She held her finger in the air to stop Henry, but the look on his face told her she needed to hurry. "My tuna casserole for the potluck after church Sunday? I'd be happy to. Got to go, Henry needs me. I'll talk to you later."

The phone barely in the cradle, Henry started. "Liza, you have to see this."

"What in the world is going on?" She followed him out to the barn, where he was digging through boxes in the back. "What are you looking for?"

"Rope. I know we have some. Can you grab a couple of buckets by the side of the barn?"

"Isn't there a hole in the bucket, Henry?" she asked smartly.

"Huh?" He gave her a blank look.

"I'll get the buckets." She walked out of the barn, mumbling under her breath. "I think you're losing it, dear Henry." Sometimes his whims and fancies amused her, but other times it was pure frustration.

"Hey, Liza." He walked out of the barn with the rope in his hand. "Do we have any apples… or carrots? I think llamas like those."

"Llamas? Have you lost your ever-loving mind?"

"Forget it. Get in the truck, Liza. You'll see."

The brothers ambled up and down the creek bed, mastering the art of quenching their thirst. At the sound of an engine, they lifted their heads, ears perked straight up. This sound was different than the one before, and they needed to see what it was.

Following the path the tractor had taken, the truck bounced over the rough terrain. Pulling the scarf snug over her head, Liza glanced at her husband. She couldn't remember the last time that fire had been in his eyes.

"Is this one of your cockamamie, crazy wild goose chases, Henry?"

He looked at her, his hair damp from sweat. "You'll see Liza, you'll see."

She hummed their old song, and he heard her whisper, "Hole in the bucket, Dear Henry, a hole."

18

"Really. You just wait and see." Bouncing off the seat as the truck hit a bump, Liza rolled her eyes, but grinned as he continued the tune. Henry slowed as they passed the old willow, his breath catching at the sadness which washed over Liza's face. Pushing her hair under the scarf, she looked at him with an understanding only profound loss can bring.

"Almost there." Henry squeezed her hand as the old truck groaned up the hill.

"Well?" Her eyes scanned the empty pasture.

"I swear there were two baby llamas here." The truck rolled to a stop and Henry turned off the engine. Getting out, he walked to where he had seen the llamas earlier but could find no sign of them.

Liza knotted the scarf under her neck and climbed out of the truck, joining him along the fence line. "Henry…"

"They were right here. A black one and a white one. The black one followed me to the tractor and tried to eat my hair. Liza. Am I losing my mind?" She wrapped her hands around his shoulders and pulled him into a hug, then looking over his shoulder, gasped.

"Henry, look."

"What?" He turned to see the llamas peeking around the edge of the trees.

"Oh, Henry, they're babies."

"They went to the creek, Liza. That's why we needed the buckets." He bolted forward, but at the sudden movement, the llamas darted back behind the trees.

Henry took Liza's hand. "Come on, we have to go and stand by the truck. Pretend we're ignoring them. Hurry." Reaching the truck, he said: "See, Liza, they're real. I'm not losing my mind."

"Not sure I'd go that far…." But the excitement was infectious, and glancing over her shoulder as they walked, she giggled as the llamas watched them.

FOUR

Liza watched with delight as the llamas emerged from the trees and approached them. The white one stopped short, causing the black one to stumble into him. Lifting his head, the white llama glowered over his shoulder at his brother, who glared back.

"Should we get in the truck?" Liza's eyes were bright with excitement.

"Nah, I don't think so," Henry started. "But on second thought…." He opened the truck door a crack. "Just in case." Grinning, he reached down and pulled bunches of grass, tucking some in her hand. "Here they come… stand still."

The white one approached first, bent its head, nuzzling the grass out of Liza's hand. Mouth pinched, she snickered, eyes squeezed shut, holding in a full bellied laugh. The black llama came up to Henry, sniffing his face, then reached for the now-familiar handful of grass.

"Hi, old friend," Henry whispered.

The white one let his head drift down to Liza's bare legs. Her eyes opened wide. "Henry."

"Hold still, Liza. He's simply curious."

"But Henry…." She squealed as the white llama nosed into the bottom of her dress, lifting it and sniffing her legs. Liza jumped, then the white llama jumped. The black llama stuck his nose into the middle as chaos erupted. "Henry, my dress!" Frantic, she tried to pull the dress loose, now tangled around the white llama's nose. A button flew off, causing her dress to billow in the air.

Henry opened the door. "Quick, climb in, Liza."

Flushed and snickering despite herself, Liza perched on the truck's step as Henry grabbed her butt and pushed her in, climbing in after. He slammed the door shut, then snorted as he saw his proper wife on all fours, scarf hanging off her head, hair a wild mess. She lowered her head, glared around, then couldn't help but join him in a fit of giggles as she righted herself on the seat. They clutched their bellies, shaking with laughter until tears streamed down their cheeks, their laughter spilling out into the world.

A wind stirred the trees on Little Sister Mountain Putucusi, carrying the laughter of Henry and Liza like echoes of an ancient song. King Llama lifted his head, a blade of grass hanging out of his mouth. His eyes glistened as they always did when joy that has been bound in sorrow is released into the world, creating healing throughout the entire universe.

Henry laughed so hard he dropped the keys on the floor. Reaching down, just as his fingers hit the cold metal of the keyring, he hit his head on the gear shaft. Liza burst out into snorts, which made him laugh harder. Sitting upright, he put the keys in the ignition, then turned to Liza and traced her face with his hand. "Oh, Liza, I can't remember when I ever had so much fun." They sat and watched the llamas watching them, neither one wanting to move and disturb the lingering magic.

"Where did they come from, Henry?"

"I don't know. I drove out here this morning, and they were there. Do you think someone would dump them? Where's the mother?" He scratched his head. "Weird."

"What are we going to tell everyone?"

"The truth," Henry said. "They just showed up. I mean, I'll call the sheriff and report it."

"And maybe that new vet would know. I think his name is Freddy?"

"Yeah. He might know if a llama in the area gave birth recently."

"Or maybe we could keep it a secret." Liza looked up with a question mark in her eyes. "I sort of like them."

He patted her hand. "We'll see, Liza. Let's head back, make a call."

The young llamas stood, perplexed, watching the truck drive away, across the grass and down the hill. They knew they had done good, but didn't understand yet that it was their mere presence that would bring great healing to Henry and Liza, whose world was about to change.

Henry slowed as they passed the giant willow with the swing hanging from an outreaching branch. He stopped the truck and turned off the key. "It's been a while." The door creaked as he opened it and stepped out. "I'll be right back." Feet making soft, crunchy sounds as they tred on dried leaves, he heard the passenger door open and turned. "Liza?"

"I imagine you could use help?"

The llamas looked at each other, then raised their noses to the sky, hoping for guidance.

Follow… stay? Curiosity insisted they follow the truck, yet an unseen force told them to stay. Distracted by patches of fragrant, tall grass, they wandered back to the fence line. Soon, they resumed their bookend positions, each gazing in opposite directions, alert for anything that might require their attention. In the warm afternoon sun, their minds drifted back to the rivers, mountains, and seas as they journeyed to this very place and let the knowledge that all would be well settle in their hearts. In the stone city of Machu Picchu, King Llama ventured into the little stone house where he found his fellow alpacas and llamas in deep meditation. They looked up at him, and he nodded his head. "All is well."

Henry reached the tree, tugged on the rope then gave the swing a little push. "Would have thought it would have rotted out by now." Liza joined him as they walked to the back of the tree. Henry ran his fingertips over the carved initials and stick figures drawn on the trunk. "The last time we were together."

"Almost ten years ago. Has it really been that long?" Liza put her arm through his and snuggled in close, reaching up and tracing the letters carved in the tree. "Oh Christopher… Jimmy…. my sons, how I miss you." Her hands traced the stick figure arm to the second stick figure. "High five," she laughed softly. "They thought it was their secret code."

"Right," Henry chuckled as he put his hand over hers, and they traced the initials JM. "I can remember that day like it was yesterday. How could they be so alike on the outside, yet so different on the inside?"

"And the day they got their draft notices," Liza started. "The looks on their faces, the fear in my heart."

"Standing right here. Chris was excited about going into the Army... he was even excited about going to Vietnam. I mean, we all knew that would happen with the draft."

"But Jimmy... another story," Liza continued. "So headstrong. Wasn't anyone going to tell him what to do."

"Last letter we got was from somewhere in Canada."

Liza sighed. "Wonder if we'll ever know what happened or if he even knows his brother died over there in Vietnam? God, I hated that war. It stole both of my sons from me."

"From us." Henry reached further up the tree trunk and traced his fingers over his own initials, HM. His stick-figure was holding a pitchfork. "Round and round we go. Seems like we keep circling back and always end up at this place where nothing is left but memories."

"Push me, Henry." Liza went and sat on the swing, which creaked under her weight.

"Liza, it's not safe."

"I don't care, Henry. I'm tired of being safe."

"But, Liza, what if the swing breaks?"

"Says the man who hasn't fixed the hole in the bucket." She looked over her shoulder at him. "Just push, Henry. I need to feel the wind in my face. I need to feel my boys."

Henry gave a hard tug on the rope and looked up at the branch holding it. "Well, seems okay. Ready, Liza?"

"Just do it, Henry."

He gave her a gentle push, watching her scarf fall around her shoulders, freeing long gray curls, which fell softly down her back as she leaned. He pushed a little harder. Liza pumped her legs and, building momentum, closed her eyes, imagining that somewhere out there, her boys were feeling it too.

Suddenly, the branch above gave a loud crack. Henry caught Liza around the waist as she swung back and held on as the branch gave way. Her feet pulled through the rope just as the branch fell on top of the swing. Together Henry and Liza hit the ground, rolling away from the crash.

"Are you okay, Liza?"

"I'm fine, Henry," she whispered, lying very still, head cradled on his shoulder, his arms tight around her.

"That was close, Liza," he murmured. "I can't lose you. I was foolish to go along with it. Liza?" Henry said, loosening his grip. "Are you sure you're okay?"

Liza freed herself and slowly sat up. "Well, I scraped my knee and elbow. No worse for the wear." She held up the bottom of her dress, torn to shreds. "Can't say the same for this dress, however."

"I'll buy you a new dress, Liza. And a new scarf." He tousled her hair. "Haven't seen you this mussed up in a long time."

"You put that twinkle right out of your eyes, Henry." But she reached up and ran her fingers along his jawline. "Thank you for catching me."

"Not sure I'll ever be the same." Henry stood and rubbed his back and hip. "But I have you." He reached down to help her up. "And we have two llamas, so it seems."

As the sun began its descent, the llamas wandered through the pasture. They made their way to the edge where earlier they watched Henry's taillights disappear over the hill, then turned to the fence line, learning the boundaries of the land. As the day neared its end,

26

they found a spot in the grass, still warm from the sunny day, and settled in like bookends as the sun sank behind the trees.

Hours later, Henry looked up as the door to the cellar opened. Liza stepped out, holding a large bag of apples and an assortment of vegetables. "You said llamas like carrots and apples, right?"

"I think so."

"We're pretty stocked up, but they'll go through it fast. Might be a good idea to move them over to the pasture with the apple and pear trees."

"Liza…"

"I know. We don't know anything about them yet."

"The sheriff didn't have a clue. Said animals get dumped all the time. Someone might have figured with this much land, we wouldn't even notice. The vet hasn't called back. Maybe he'll know."

"Do you remember the man who talked about having llamas after church last week?"

"They were new."

"I'll call Helen. She'll know."

Henry rolled his eyes. "Yes, Helen knows everything…."

"I know, I know…" Liza said. "Helen's Helen. But you know what Henry? Even though our community was good to us during our hard times, Helen, in her busybody way, didn't miss a beat… always checking on us, bringing hot meals, finding ways to make sure we were okay. She carries her own cross."

At the sound of the phone, they hurried into the house. Liza grabbed the phone off the cradle. Henry squeezed in next to her, and she cupped the phone so they both could listen, excited to hear the voice of the vet, Freddy.

"Humph…" Henry said as Liza hung up the phone. "He doesn't know of any llamas ready to give birth or how they could possibly end up here."

"And he'll come out tomorrow to have a look. Henry, I really like the llamas."

"I know, Liza. Me too." He sat down on the kitchen chair. "For the first time since the boys left, I feel excited about tomorrow."

"We'll head out there first thing in the morning."

"Henry, don't you think we should bring them into the barn? They're babies, and it's going to get cold out there."

"Let's see what tomorrow brings. And what the vet says."

"What shall we name them, Henry?"

"I don't know." Henry stood and unbuckled the straps on his overalls. "So much has happened today. Let's sleep on it."

"Oh, I hope I can sleep." Liza rubbed her knee, now swollen and red.

"How about I run a bath for you? A good soak might help that knee."

"Yes, let's do that." Liza busied herself cleaning up their dinner dishes.

Minutes later, with sounds of water running into the tub, Henry stuck his head out. "Your bath is ready. Tossed a handful of epsom salts in there."

"Thank you, Henry. It'll feel good."

Patiently he waited as she undressed, then steadied her as she stepped into the steaming water. Looking up, she said: "First thing tomorrow, right Henry?"

FIVE

Early the next morning, Henry was surprised to wake up to the smell of coffee drifting through the bedroom door. Scratching his head, and other parts here and there, he crawled out of bed and looked out of the window, the sky tinged with pinks and grays of the coming sunrise. Sore from the fall they took yesterday, he rubbed his back as he shuffled to the kitchen. Liza stood at the sink looking out the window, drumming her fingers on the countertop. Her old overalls were rolled up at the bottom and two long braids hung down her back. Leaning against the door jam, he smiled. She could still make his heart skip a beat.

"No dress today?" Chuckling, he reached up to the cupboard, then looked down and saw their two red, coffee-stained mugs sitting next to the percolator, brown liquid drops rising and falling in the glass top. A carton of cream sat next to them.

Liza looked over her shoulder and grinned at him, standing in his faded long johns. "Coffees about done. Better get dressed, Henry, we've got things to do." He looked at the bag of apples and carrots by the back door.

"Right." He turned and went into the bedroom, pausing at the tall dresser. Bending to the bottom drawer, Henry rubbed his hip, the usual ache that reminded him he was still alive. Pulling out a fresh pair of overalls, the door jammed as he closed it, causing the picture on top of the dresser to fall. Catching it mid-air, he stumbled, dropped the overalls on the floor and sat down heavily on the bed, the picture cradled in his hands. It was Chris and Jimmy at their high school graduation. Even though they were identical twins, they couldn't have been more different. Chris had always kept his hair trimmed, face clean shaven, while Jimmy sported a mustache and goatee, his hair slicked back in a ponytail. Henry ran his fingers over the picture. Both boys had been happy growing up, evident by the sparkle in their eyes. Jimmy had more of a smirk, and his not always funny pranks were memorable. As they got older, Chris became a rule follower, always polite and caring. Jimmy, however, spoke his truth, often before thinking it through, whether one wanted to hear it or not. But they had both been kind, popular on the football team and hopeful of a full ride college scholarship. But all that changed when the draft notices came. And now, eleven years later, both of their sons were gone. Chris, dead in Vietnam and Jimmy, off somewhere in Canada. Dead, alive? He had no idea. They hadn't had a word in over seven years. Henry stood and put the picture back on the dresser, tucking away the grief that was always nearby, ready to say hello. He pulled the overalls over his white tee shirt and slipped the clasps over the metal buttons. Out of the top drawer, he pulled out a pair of clean wool socks, glancing one more time at the picture before turning to greet the day.

Standing on the grassy plaza in the stone city of Machu Picchu, King Llama gazed across the gorge at Little Sister Mountain Putucusi. Soft white clouds draped around her, a gentle shroud whispering ancient secrets. Unlike the jagged peaks of other mountains, Putucusi was soft and round, with arms that reached out as if to offer comfort.

As sun's first light broke through the clouds, she greeted her old friend. King Llama lowered himself to his knees and slowly allowed his hindquarters to rest on the earth. "Today's the day." He raised his nose to the sky, eyes closing, as if listening to a distant call.

Little Sister Mountain Putucusi smiled, blowing an invisible hug that wrapped around her King Llama, filling him with peace. The world held its breath, for the moment had come, and all that was would soon change.

"Hurry, Henry." Liza went to the back of the old blue Chevy pickup. The rusty pin screeched as she pulled the latch free, pushed it aside and lowered the tailgate. Laughing, she removed the two buckets she had thrown in the back yesterday, not knowing at the time what was to come. Picking them up, she dangled them by their rope handles and humming, turned to Henry.

"There's a hole in the bucket, dear Henry, dear Henry.
There's a hole in the bucket, dear Henry, a hole."

"That's my line." But he grinned and took the buckets from her, tossing them next to the barn.

Liza put the apples and carrots on the bed of the pickup. "Do you think we need hay or straw? It gets cold overnight… they're so young."

"The vet is coming this afternoon. We'll ask." Henry opened the driver's side door. "I can order it from the feed store if we need it. Ooops, forgot the keys. Hop in, I'll be right back."

Henry plucked the keys off the hook on the inside of the back door and as he was walking away, heard the phone ring. Pausing, he thought about going in and answering, but then Liza leaned out of the truck, her expression impatient. Shrugging, Henry ignored his curiosity and walked toward the truck.

At the other end of the line, the man in the phone booth hung up and shook his head no to the woman. "We'll try again later. Let's hit the road."

Just before sunrise, a mother fox and her kits ran through the pasture, their swift movements making the tall grass whisper and sway. The soft rustling teased the young llama's noses, making them twitch in surprise. The white one scrunched up his face and looked over at the black one, who was doing the same.

As the mother fox scolded her young, the llama's eyes widened in alarm. Instinct calling them to action, they rose together, their gazes locked on the shifting grass, now concealing the fox family within its folds. Despite wobbly legs, the white llama took a determined step forward, his spirit unwavering.

Suddenly, one of the kits broke free from its mother's side, sprinting back through the meadow, dancing in circles around the black llama. Startled, the llama pinned his ears back, lifted his nose, and with a great rush of energy, released a burst of green liquid from his stomach. The kit froze, eyes wide with surprise, then, sensing danger, scampered back to its mother. The mama fox, her family in tow, hurried them out of the pasture, leaving behind only whispering grass and lingering echoes of the moment.

Both llamas raised their heads, ears perked high, proud that they had been brave and protected the land. They spent the morning walking the fence line, then made their way down to the creek, where they practiced slurping water and holding their heads high, letting the cold liquid stream down their throats. At mid swallow, the sound of an engine made them look up. Time to go.

Two hundred miles to the North, at a café near Cougar Falls, Washington, Katherine reached across the table and touched Jimmy's hand, which held down the corner of a map. "How long till we get there?"

"Four to five hours," he mumbled, running his fingers through his hair, which had grown to the middle of his back. He looked up at his wife. "How are you doing?"

"Other than feeling like I have to pee every five minutes, I'm okay." She smiled and squeezed his hand.

Jimmy leaned across the table and gave her a lingering kiss but pulled away to the sound of a woman clearing her throat. "Sorry," he said to the waitress, who smirked as she set their baskets with burgers and fries on the table. "We're having a baby. I'm excited... can't help it."

"That's nice," the waitress said, her smirk turning to a smile as she turned and walked away.

"You never lose your charm, eh Jimmy?" Katherine grinned at him.

"Are we doing the right thing, Katherine? I mean, President Carter just granted amnesty to draft dodgers, but what if there's a catch? I don't want to cause problems for the folks."

"No problems at the border."

"I was lost up there on that mountain, Katherine. If it hadn't been for the flat tire on your delivery truck, I might have never come down."

"I would have gotten that tire fixed. Eventually." She took a bite out of her burger, grinning at him. "Admit it, you couldn't resist me."

"Right... "Jimmy chuckled. "But seriously, I want this to be right."

On their way out of the diner, Jimmy handed the waitress a ten-dollar bill. "Keep the change." He winked at her.

The waitress, who had become jaded over time, softened, not believing her luck at the generous tip. "Thank you, sir." Waving the bill in her hand, she looked up as Katherine came out of the bathroom. "Good luck with your baby!"

"You're spending money like we have it, eh?"

"It's all good." Jimmy smoothed his hand over her thick, curly braid, letting his fingers linger in the wispy curls at the bottom. She didn't know about the wad of cash he had as a back-up, generated from marijuana he had grown and sold in Canada.

Bouncing along in the truck, Liza nudged Henry with her elbow.

**"There's a hole in the bucket,
Dear Henry, Dear Henry.
There's a hole in the bucket, Dear Henry, a hole."**

"Then fix it Dear Liza…" Henry started in, then stopped. "You becoming all women's libber on me Liza?" He glanced over, a grin forming. "That's the second time today you stole my line. I'm supposed to be the one telling you there's a hole in the bucket. I grew up with that song, I ought to know." He watched her out of the corner of his eye with a pouty look on his face but a twinkle in his eyes.

"Maybe we've had it wrong all along. If I had just fixed that dang hole in the bucket…"

"Ah, Liza." He slowed as they went by the willow. "How's your knee today?"

"A little sore." She mused. "But it was worth it."

Approaching the top of the hill, they saw two heads peeking out of the trees on the other side of the pasture.

"Look, they're waiting for us."

King Llama, grazing on the ancient stair-stepped terraces of Machu Picchu, looked up as Little Sisters Mountain Putucusi's giggle drifted across the air. A smile tugged on his lips as he whispered: "It's a beautiful thing when a divine plan falls into place."

Taking a deep, knowing breath, Little Sister Mountain Putucusi expanded her arms ever so slightly, revealing a hidden cave within her belly, revealing a shadowed figure inside.

King Llama's expression softened as his gaze lingered on the figure with reverence and joy, understanding the deep magic of the moment, when time and destiny align in a single, perfect breath.

Henry shoved the truck into reverse, wrinkling his face at the grinding of the gears. "Someday I'll learn to drive," he said to Liza's frown. He backed up the hill, about halfway into the pasture. "Here we go."

Parking brake pulled up, he stepped out of the truck and walked around to open Liza's door. But she had beat him to it and was already at the back of the truck, working the pin out of the latch. Tailgate down, Henry pulled an old milk crate out of the back, and using it as a step, gave his wife a hand up into the bed of the truck and climbed in after her. Settled, they put the bags of apples and carrots between them, then waited. The llamas edged their way out of the trees, eyes big with curiosity and ears perked high as they moved towards the truck.

"We need names for them, Henry."

"How about Bacardi for the white one? He seems in charge, a little more cautious, less impulsive than the other one."

"Bacardi? Why Bacardi?"

"Sort of like the famous rum. Smooth, light bodied, easy on your stomach, good for your spirit." Henry grinned at her. "A survivor, yet good natured."

"Hmmm…." She frowned. "But what would our friends say… naming a llama after alcohol?"

"You're tired of playing it safe, remember?" He pinched her chin playfully. "It'll be a scandal. I can see it now."

"I like it." Liza grinned at him. "But Helen…"

"Ah, Helen. That makes it all worthwhile."

She gave him a punch in the arm. "That woman might surprise you."

"I'll be a fly on the wall for that story."

"How about Domingo for the black one?" Liza mused. "Dark, mysterious and a bit impulsive. A lover of adventure. You can see it in his eyes."

They looked up as the llamas approached. Giggling, she reached into the bag, placing two carrots in one hand and an apple in the other.

Henry grabbed carrots out of the bag. "Now, be still."

The llamas sniffed the air around them, the fenders of the truck, then the black llama moved to Liza and nosed her shoes, nibbling on the laces of her tennies. She squirmed. He looked up, sniffed her hair, gave a soft snort that felt like a powder puff on her cheek. She giggled as he delicately took the small, green apple out of her hand, breaking it in two on the first crunch. On impulse, she reached out and touched him, smoothing her hand along his neck from the bottom of his ears to his chest. "So soft," she whispered. "Domingo, you're so soft."

Henry looked over and mumbled: "You always had the touch with the young ones." The white llama stood back, watching… but unable to contain his curiosity, came forward, nuzzling the carrots out of Henry's hand. "Tongue as smooth as Bacardi rum."

King Llama and Little Sister Mountain Putucusi smiled as they watched friendships form. Fifty miles to the north of the farm, Jimmy turned on the signal, prepared to turn down the county road, which led home. A home he wondered if he would ever see again. Katherine scooted over and snuggled. "All will be well," she whispered, kissing him on the cheek. "I can feel it."

Henry looked at the sky, then at the llamas, who had wandered back out into the pasture. "Almost midday." He put his hat on and jumped down, offering Liza a hand. "Be careful of your knee."

As they arrived back at the house, the vet pulled up in his Wagoneer. Freddy's handshake was strong despite his slight build. "You had a couple of llamas show up?"

"Yep," Henry said. "I went out on the tractor yesterday morning and they were hanging out in the upper pasture. Sheriff said someone might have dumped them." He shrugged. "It's a mystery. But they're welcome here if no one claims them."

"Well, let's see 'em."

Liza walked out of the barn with a rope coiled in her hand. "My wife, Liza," Henry said. "I think we'll all fit in the truck."

"I'm good in the back." Freddy grabbed his medical bag out of the Jeep and tossed it in the bed of the pickup, then jumped in after it.

SIX

King Llama knelt on the ancient terrace, his eyes following the vast gorge between him and Little Sister Mountain Putucusi. His gaze sank into the depths below, where memories, woven over countless ages, flowed through his mind like a river. Endless, timeless, deep. Lifting his head, he looked once more to Little Sister Mountain Putucusi, her trees sparkling in the afternoon light.

She smiled in her quiet, eternal way, and with a subtle, graceful motion, parted just enough to allow light to pour into the hidden cave nestled within the curve of her arms. The figure inside shifted as it became more defined. The moment they had long awaited. The earth held its breath, the heavens paused, and the whispers of destiny echoed in the winds that danced between them.

Freddy opened his face to the fresh air. Nostalgic for his roots in San Francisco at times, the rolling hills and lush landscape of Oregon, especially after the rain, invigorated him. He chuckled at the phone call with his mother yesterday.

"Are you having fun, Bobo?" she asked. "Met anyone yet?"

New in town, Freddy was excited to receive a call from the farmer about the llamas. When Ken, the old, retiring veterinarian took him on, people were skeptical of a newcomer, but slowly the community was warming to him. Raised in the heart of a bustling city with hippie lawyer parents, involved in politics and the social scene of San Francisco, Freddy often tired of the noise and constant motion. Eager to show him the world, his parents had taken him to faraway places his friends hadn't even heard of. But those travels left him longing for open spaces and endless blue skies. He liked this town, and he loved animals.

"Yeah, Mom, remember that trip to Peru and the llama? I think I was eight?"

"Oh, Bobo, you just stood there and let that llama get in your face. I thought that dangerous animal would knock you right off that mountain."

Freddy laughed. "I wasn't scared. In fact, tomorrow I'm going to check out a couple of baby llamas that showed up on an old farmer's land. Maybe you can meet them when you visit."

Freddy jolted back into reality as they bounced over the root of the old willow tree. Grabbing his bag as it slid across the truck bed, he glanced over at the swing hanging from a giant willow, dangling by a thread, wondering what memories it held. Curious, he stretched his neck around, taking in the lush pasture as the farmer eased the truck into the field, wheels crunching over the grass. Their excitement infectious, Freddy couldn't deny a stirring within him. It was like a cord sprang out from deep inside him, linking his core to the earth and heavens, connecting him to his destiny. He couldn't wait to tell his mom.

King Llama trembled, his spirit alight with the electricity of the moment. The trees on Little Sister Mountain Putucusi fluttered in response, her leaves shimmering as if the very heartbeat of Mother Earth joined with theirs.

It seemed only a breath ago he gazed into the eyes of the young boy, seeing with perfect clarity the future healer who stood before him that day. He knew these moments often got lost in the chaos of everyday living, but like a forgotten star shining through the veil of clouds, innate understanding occasionally shines through, allowing the individual to remember. His heart swelled, brimming with gratitude for the young man who embraced his destiny, allowing it to unfold in perfect time.

Freddy jumped out and, eager to meet the llamas, jogged up the hill. The llamas turned and ran towards the trees.

"Whoa, partner." Henry called out. "I don't want to tell you how to do your business, but we found if we stay by the truck and keep these apples close, they'll come to us."

"Ah, dang it. I know better." Freddy smiled at Henry, tossing his medical bag in the cab.

They arranged themselves on the tailgate, avoided looking at the llamas and chattered softly. "I have the rope handy," Henry murmured. He met Freddy's eyes, smiling at the excitement, then turned and caught Liza's nod of approval.

Soon, Domingo crept closer, sniffing around the fender well before stretching his long neck toward Liza's braid and giving it a curious nibble. She stifled a giggle, then, with a grin, reached behind her back and offered the carrot in her hand. Intrigued, Domingo took it and stepped closer, nosing into her shirt. Liza snorted, then burst into laughter. Domingo backed off and stood looking at her, ears perked. He didn't sense danger, and he liked carrots. The woman's tone and laughter felt safe, but he'd never been in this situation. Really, he hadn't been in any situation before. Everything was new. He glanced over at his brother for advice.

Freddy tensed with excitement as the white llama stepped closer. He could almost reach out and touch the soft, downy curls on his chest. *His?* How did he know? In his youth, the phrase *right time, right place* had been tossed around often, but now, for the first time, he truly understood. An unseen thread seemed to be weaving a new path. Henry slipped an apple into his hand. With a grateful nod, Freddy held it out. As Bacardi's velvet tongue brushed the fruit, their eyes met - curious, steady. And just like that, Freddy was eight years old again, staring into the gaze of a llama so similar, yet older and larger. A guardian from another time.

SEVEN

Jimmy pulled into the old Standard station on the outskirts of town. He was surprised when old Max stepped out of the building. As far back as he could remember, Max had been old, and ten years hadn't done him any favors. Max limped over to the car as Jimmy opened the door and got out.

"Oh my God!" Max wrapped Jimmy in a hug. "Where the hell you been boy?"

"Canada."

Max shook his head, sadness filling his eyes.

"Sorry about your brother, boy."

"Sorry? Brother?" Jimmy's stomach grew cold.

Surprise and regret filled Max's face. "You didn't know."

"Know what?" Katherine stuck her head out of the driver's side window. "Know what, eh?" she repeated to the men's stunned faces.

"Chris…" Max lowered his head, his voice a whisper. "He was killed over there in that Vietnam."

Jimmy doubled over, holding himself up on the hood of his car. With her large pregnant belly, Katherine wedged out the door and went over, folding her arms around him.

"I'm sorry," Max stammered. "I thought…"

"No." Jimmy put his hand on Max's shoulder and shook his head. "I shouldn't be surprised." He stood, breath heaving in and out of his chest. "How are the folks?"

"It's been hard for them." Max fumbled with the gas cap. "They're getting on. Got rid of the cattle a couple of years ago. Couldn't keep up." Katherine remained silent, knowing no words could make it better. "But one thing's for sure."

"What's that, Max?" Jimmy asked.

"You're going to be a sight for sore eyes." He hung up the gas nozzle and replaced the cap, wiping his hands on pin-striped coveralls. "Now get going home, boy. Gas is on the house."

Back in the car, as they drove out, Jimmy stuck his head out of the window. "Thanks, Max."

"Welcome home, boy!" Max took off his cap, waving it in the air. "Now get going!"

Freddy sat with Henry and Liza on the tailgate, watching the young llamas as they wandered back to the tree line, positioning themselves so they could watch over the entire pasture. Somehow, they knew protecting this land, including the humans, was their responsibility. They would keep an eye on what they were up to.

"They look healthy," Freddy said, scratching his head. "You haven't seen any people around or unusual activity?"

"Nope." Henry glanced out of the corner of his eyes at Liza. "Checked with the sheriff. News to him."

"Won't they be cold out here?" Liza leaned around Henry, touching Freddy's arm. "They're so young. They could come in the barn.""

"Start parking the truck further away each time you come out. Draw them in." He laughed. "Can't believe this. When I was a boy,

I went to Peru with my folks. On Machu Picchu, I saw a llama up close. Looked just like the white one."

"Bacardi," Liza said. "You mean Bacardi, the white llama."

"Yes, Bacardi," Freddy chuckled. "Maybe it was his ancestor… stared me right in the eye. I didn't realize it at the time, but I think that's when I decided to become a vet."

Henry jerked his head around. "Interesting. And you just happened to pick our town to settle in." Liza met his gaze with a knowing smile.

"Mind if I come out again tomorrow?"

"We'd love that. I'll have the coffee ready." Liza smiled. "Breakfast, too, if you're hungry."

"Most likely." Freddy said. "The llamas will want to stay here where they can see everything. But they might come down, never know."

"We could build a shelter out here," Henry said. "And on the other side of this pasture, there's an orchard with apple and pear trees. Put 'em to good use."

Freddy jumped down off the tailgate and got his bag out of the cab, opening it. "I'd like to get my hands on them, make sure they're healthy, deworm them. But that can wait. We don't want to scare them away."

"Can we keep them?" Liza's face tightened with anxiety.

"Unless someone makes a legitimate claim, you just became llama owners."

"Legitimate claim?" Henry asked.

"If someone can show me a llama who recently gave birth, and explain how they got here on your property, I'd have to listen. But I doubt that happening." He smiled as Liza's face relaxed. "I'll tell the sheriff as well." He dug around in his bag. "I'll gather the injections they'll need. No rush. We might need a little more muscle. I'll ask around if anyone's looking for work."

Freddy jumped up into the bed of the truck as Henry and Liza got in the cab. The llamas looked up as the engine started. They perked up their ears in interest but, used to the sound now, relaxed, resuming their book-end positions along the tree line.

At the farmhouse, Henry patted the vet on his back, letting his hand rest for a moment.

"Till tomorrow?"

Freddy got in his Jeep and stuck his head out the window. "See ya first thing."

Driving away, Freddy said a prayer of thanks. The peace he felt on the mountain of Machu Picchu, always tucked quietly in his heart, stirred to life, quickening his heartbeat. Nearing the main road, he was surprised to see a car, paused with its blinker flashing, ready to turn down the driveway. Wondering who they were, he gave a friendly wave as he turned.

Jimmy slowed as he passed Freddy's Jeep, paling as if he'd seen a ghost.

"Who was that?" Katherine asked.

Jimmy shook his head. "Fifteen minutes ago, I would have said my brother."

She reached over and took his hand. "Guess it'll take time to settle in."

He slowed the car to a stop. "Is this too much? Should we turn around?"

Smiling, she pinched his cheek. "Eh? We've come this far."

"You're right." Jimmy put the car into gear. "Plus, once they're over the shock, mom will go nuts over the idea of having a grandbaby."

Henry and Liza busied themselves in the barn, clearing a spot for the llamas. "If we can get them down here," Henry said, "they'll know this is a warm, safe place when the cold rolls in." He went over to a stack of two by fours. "Could use these to build a shelter for them."

Liza peered over his shoulder.

"Ready to get into all this again, Liza?" His hands traced her braids.

She grinned. "I love seeing that spark back in your eyes again, Henry. But remember…"

"I know," he laughed. "There's a hole in the bucket." They turned at the sound of a car coming down the driveway. "Freddy forget something?"

"Wonder who it is?" Henry shielded his eyes with his hand. "Don't know anyone who drives a Plymouth Fury. Can't see the plates… hey, Liza, can you?"

"Too much dust." They watched the black car coming down the driveway. "Someone's probably lost… You don't think it's about the llamas, do you, Henry?" A frown worked its way across her forehead.

"Guess we'll find out soon enough."

EIGHT

The woman in the passenger seat reached over and hugged the driver, then opened the door and eased her pregnant belly out, standing.

"Hi, I'm Katherine. Old Max at the gas station said my driver would be a sight for your sore eyes, eh?" She leaned into the car. "Come on out now."

Henry and Liza stood frozen as the driver opened the door and stepped out, his head slowly rising above the roof of the car, looking over at them.

Liza gasped.

"Jimmy?" Henry whispered, putting his arm around his wife's shoulders in case she fainted.

Jimmy stood, his eyes resting on his parents. In a rush of emotion, he hurried around the car and gathered them into his arms. "Mom, Pop." His voice cracked.

Liza cupped his face with her hands, staring. "It's really you, Jimmy."

"Yes. We made plans to come as soon as we got the news that Carter pardoned draft dodgers."

"We?" Henry looked past Jimmy to Katherine, still standing near the car.

"Oh." He pulled his parents over. "Mom, Pop, this is my wife, Katherine. We're having a baby." His face turned red. "Guess it's obvious."

Liza stood looking at them, face pale. Jimmy caught her as her knees started to buckle.

Henry glanced over, ensuring Jimmy had his mom, then took Katherine's arm and ushered her towards the back door. "Let's go inside, young lady. That's a heavy load you're carrying."

Jimmy stayed back for a moment, holding her. "Mom," was all he could mutter before his voice broke again. He pulled her into his arms and hugged her. "I've missed you, Mom."

Liza couldn't control the tears as they streamed down her face. "We tried to find you, Jimmy. Had no idea…"

"I was up in the mountains…."

"I need to tell you…" Her blue eyes filled with a fresh batch of tears. "Chris…"

"Old Max at the gas station told me. I'm sorry, Mom. I'm sure you'd rather it was Chris standing here."

"Jimmy, no!" Liza gripped his arms, her face a blaze of fury. "Why didn't you write? Tell us you were okay?"

"I'm sorry. I was lost up in the mountains. There were rumors the government was monitoring the mail, and I didn't want to cause any trouble for you."

"You're here now." Liza took hold of his shoulders, turning him in a full circle. Satisfied, she cupped his chin in her hands. "And you are married." Her eyes grew wide. "I'm going to be a grandma?"

"Yes, Mom." Jimmy said. "Yes, you are. Come on, you'll love Katherine."

✩
✩

As Domingo and Bacardi settled in for the evening and the sun dipped behind the tall pines, it felt like they'd been in the pasture far longer than just two days. Their legs were stronger, and they stood taller.

Far away on a mountaintop, as the waning light glistened on peaks, valleys, and rivers, King Llama held his head high. His reign was nearing its end, and one day another would take his place, but for now, King Llama had never felt more honored to be a part of something so good.

Little Sister Mountain Putucusi expanded with her breath. The figure in the cave stood and came out to the edge. Even though it was only a shadow, the army fatigues, and beret on his head were clear, rainbow light illuminating in waves. Since he died in Vietnam, he watched over his parents, his brother, and his true love...

The timing seemed perfect. With the war coming to an end, Chris was eager to bring Claud home to meet the family. His attention drifted to a small living room in a beachfront apartment in San Diego. She was going through boxes, but like a magnet, she rose and went onto the balcony as the night's first star appeared. He reached out to touch her, only wisps of color streaming into the night sky, remembering their first kiss, under that same star.

Claud... oh Claud... what might have been...

They met at Bien Hoa Airbase in Vietnam. He was sitting on the tarmac in an Army Jeep when lightning struck. The next thing he knew, he was opening his eyes to her standing above him.

"Hey, soldier!" she said, her smile bright and contagious. Despite the wooziness that filled his head, he grinned at her. "Welcome back," she said.

"Who are you?"

"*Your angel,*" *she teased.* "*But my friends call me Claud.*" *As she turned away, he glanced around the makeshift Army hospital tent, then back at her, his eyes stopping at the snug fatigues on her bottom as she talked to the soldier next to him.*

"*Hey, what about me?*" *He called out.* "*I might be dying.*" *He heard her laugh before she turned back to him.* "*What is Claud short for?*" *he asked, lost in her blue eyes.*

"*Claudette.*" *She laughed, putting a blood pressure cuff on his arm.* "*My mom loves all things beautiful and creative, and extraordinary.*"

"*I can see that. Ouch! That's tight.*"

"*Oh, come on. You're a soldier!*" *She turned to the man behind her, moaning on the cot, then back to Chris.* "*But I think you're gonna live.*" *Unwrapping the cuff from his arm, she hung it on a hook.* "*You're good to go.*" *At the sound of retching, she grabbed a basin just as the soldier in the next bed vomited.*

Later that week, he saw her in the make-shift tent which served as the commissar. Her long blonde hair, tucked under a cap earlier, hung in loose braids down her back. Sneaking around a rack of tee shirts, he got on the other side and reached through. "*Boo.*"

She feigned surprise. "*Soldier, is that the best you got? I saw you a mile away.*"

With a look of rejection, he glanced out of the corner of his eye and then, giving her one of the famous Muller smiles, invited her to lunch. From that day on, they were inseparable, their relationship quickly developing into love with an intensity that only war can bring.

"*Marry me? When this is over?*"

"*Will it ever be over?*" *She pondered.*

"*The minute our feet touch the ground in San Diego… we'll find a minister.*"

"*Are you sure?*" *She gazed up, seeing a love in his eyes that made her head spin.*

"*I've never been surer of anything.*"

Sitting on her living room floor, the sounds of waves in the distance washed through Claud. The box she'd avoided sat in front of her. Two days after his proposal, she stood in formation, with the stoic face of a soldier, saluting as his casket rolled by, silent tears running down her cheeks. Rumors of the war ending were rampant, and they'd been excited about their future. But one last mortar shell attack on the base caught Chris and two other soldiers early one morning as they laced up their boots and prepared for the first plane of the day. Looking into the box, she pulled out his pack. Not wanting to face it, she had stashed everything away, including memories.

Hands trembling, she unzipped the pack, picking up letters that fell out. The envelopes were addressed to Henry and Liza Muller in Oregon. Feeling like an intruder, but now desperate to feel him, even if it was ink on paper, she opened the first letter:

Dear Dad and Mom

It's been a while. Sometimes it's hard to know what to write. Every day is the same… planes come in with supplies and leave, often loaded with bodies. I've lost track of how many. Near my bunk, I've made friends with a pet spider. Weirdly, knowing it's there comforts me as I fall asleep.

I can't wait to come home. Rumors are that the war is ending soon. I'll believe it when I see it but welcome the day. I miss the green pastures, the old willow tree, washing my face in the creek. How's Jimmy? How are you all doing? It will be a good day and God's blessing when I step on our land again.

But I have news…

Tears streamed down Claud's face as she read on…

I met someone. Her name is Claudette, but she goes by Claud. I believe I have found love like you have, Mom and Dad. She's a little taller than me and has long, blonde hair that's usually tucked under her Army cap. We met in the medic tent. Lightning hit my truck, and I woke to her beautiful face smiling down on me. And she doesn't put up with any crap, so I'm behaving myself. We want to marry the second our feet touch the ground stateside. And then I'll bring her home to meet you.

I can't wait! The future is bright and my heart overflows with love as I write this. Say hi to Jimmy. Tell him he's not missing anything…
All My Love, Chris

Oh, my love… Nothing mattered more to Chris than one more hour with her, to feel the softness of her skin, to tell her one more time. But each day, his body turned more to stardust, the illusion of his former shape slowly fading.

Chris gazed into his boyhood home. His parent's laughter and the joy of Jimmy's return permeated the universe, meeting the wisps of color streaming from his fingertips. He longed to reach out and touch them, but with that no longer possible, he let his love flow through the two baby llamas, like a signal, clear and steady, waiting to be tuned in like a favorite radio station.

As King Llama reminded him earlier, remaining stagnant serves no purpose. Everyone's soul journey is ongoing, including his.

NINE

"Nothing much has changed," Jimmy said, looking around the kitchen. "You're still using the same old percolator?" He chuckled and turned to Katherine. "Chris and I got him that old coffee pot when we were fourteen. Can't believe it still works."

Liza went to the cupboard and put the red mugs that said DAD and MOM on them, next to the coffee pot. "They'll be ready bright and early."

"Oh, man. The coffee mugs." Jimmy went over and hugged his mom. "You still have them!" He made a face at Katherine. "They still have them."

"Yep." Henry sat down at the kitchen table. "Drink our morning coffee in 'em every day." He turned to his new daughter-in-law. "And what about you, young lady? Is my boy treating you well?"

"Well…" Laughter danced in her eyes. "Yeah, he does all right, eh?" She slipped her hand into Jimmy's, pulling him closer, her gaze lifting to meet his, then drifting over to Henry. "He's got your sparkle in his eyes. I haven't seen it before today."

"When's your baby due?" Liza asked, sitting down in the spare chair, then jumped up. "Oh, what was I thinking? You must be starving! Let me start dinner. Still like spaghetti and meatballs, son?"

"No one makes better spaghetti than Mom," Jimmy told Katherine.

"Spaghetti it is." Liza pulled out a pot from a lower cupboard.

Katherine cleared her throat. "And to answer your question, our baby is due in two weeks."

The spoon Liza was holding clattered to the floor. She turned to Katherine. "Two weeks?"

Katherine smiled. "Yes," looking up as Jimmy and Henry wandered into the other room.

"We'll make an appointment with the doctor tomorrow," Liza said, noticing the smile disappeared from Katherine's face. "Oh, I'm sorry. Being a bossy mother-in-law already."

"We don't have insurance or anything. And I was hoping for a home birth."

"Don't you worry about the insurance thing." Liza set the spoon down and sat next to Katherine. "Around these parts we work those things out. And home birth? I've heard ladies at church talking about that. We have lots of room here and well, why not?" She touched her shoulder and smiled. "The important thing is, you're here now. You're family."

"My parents died a few years back. It's all been a little overwhelming." She wiped a tear away with her sleeve and took Liza's hand. "Thank you. Jimmy told me how kind you are."

Henry opened the door to the boy's old room. "Nothing's changed. I think you might still have clothes in the closet. We never lost hope, Jimmy."

Jimmy froze as he entered his old bedroom. The last time he'd been in this room, Chris was alive, sleeping next to him. A stuffed tiger, the mascot of their football team, still sat on his bed.

Walking over, he opened the closet door and touched the two orange and black jackets hanging on the wooden pegs, tracing the raised letters on the back that spelled 'TIGERS.' "Those were the days, huh Pop?"

"Yes, son. Those were the days." Jimmy met Henry's gaze.

"Thought you'd like to see your room for old time's sake. You and Katherine will be more comfortable in the guest room for now." Reaching over he pushed the button on the wall, turning off the light. "Your old room would be perfect for a nursery."

"We don't want to be a burden, Pop."

"Don't be ridiculous. You and Katherine are welcome here." He put his arm around Jimmy. "Let's unload your car. I smell dinner cooking. And then I'll bet you two are ready for some shut eye."

Above the kitchen sink, the window steamed over as Liza strained the spaghetti noodles.

"Almost done," she said, stirring the sauce. "Lucky for you I put away sauce and meatballs for a special occasion." Liza grinned at Jimmy.

"Why doesn't that surprise me?" Jimmy chuckled.

"Man, we haven't had a spread like this in a long time." Henry sat down and pulled his chair up.

"You're not exactly skin and bones, my dear Henry."

"Oh…" Henry turned to Jimmy. "Wait for it."

"There's that hole in the bucket…" Liza smiled, turning back to the sauce.

Jimmy burst out laughing. "You still sing that crazy song?"

"Yep," Henry chuckled. "And there's still a hole in the bucket." The old house warmed at the happiness it missed.

"When we were growing up," Jimmy told Katherine. "They used to sing this old German folk song. It goes on and on, and on…." He closed his eyes and made snoring sounds.

"Eh? I'd love to hear it." Katherine said

"Oh, trust me," Jimmy said. "You will."

Soft chatter, punctuated by laughter and snorts, filled the air.

"You must be tired," Liza said. "Settle in and I'll get the kitchen cleaned up. Oh!" She turned to Henry. "Freddy. The llamas. I forgot."

"Freddy? Llamas?" Jimmy asked.

"I was so excited to see you, I plumb forgot! Henry took the old tractor out to the upper pasture yesterday and there were two baby llamas."

"Sprung out of thin air, like magic." Henry shook his head. "Wow. A lot has happened in the last twenty-four hours.

"Freddy is the new vet in town," Liza said, her face flushed. "He stopped by today and checked them out. "We're going to keep them."

"Must have been who we passed on the driveway," Katherine said.

Liza went to the cupboard and got out three more coffee mugs. "We're going to need two pots of coffee tomorrow." She turned to Jimmy and Katherine. "Freddy is coming for breakfast."

An hour later, Jimmy lay in bed next to Katherine, who fell asleep as soon as her head hit the pillow. Through the window, he gazed at the full moon rising over the trees and thought about his twin. He wasn't surprised Vietnam took him, but it hadn't quite sunk in. They'd been born a part of each other, and now? Staring at the moon, he saw a bright star appear above it, wondering if somewhere out in the universe, his brother might be looking at the same star. With that thought in mind, holding his wife in his arms, a peace came over him, and he closed his eyes…. and in another space and time, on the cliffside of Little Sister Mountain Putucusi, Chris sat, gazing at the same moon and the same star.

Henry stood at the bedroom window with his arms around Liza. "What a day." Together they gazed up at the moon.

"You can say that again." She sighed. "Oh, Henry, can you believe it? Jimmy's home."

"And we're going to have a grandbaby." He squeezed her shoulders. "Yesterday we wondered what would become of this place. Of us. Life can sure change on a dime."

She reached around and pinched him.

"Ouch." He rubbed his arm, feigning shock.

"I'd pinch myself to see if this is all real, but I have you." She grinned and turned, melting into his arms. "Oh, Henry. What did we ever do to be so blessed?"

TEN

"Your hair is beautiful, Katherine." The percolator made glug-glug sounds as Liza brushed her daughter-in-law's long hair.

"Thanks." She closed her eyes. "Feels heavenly."

Liza smiled at Katherine's serene face. "This house hasn't seen this much activity in… well since Chris and Jimmy left." Liza parted her hair. "If you're coming to see the llamas, we'll need to braid your hair. The llamas like to eat hair, especially that Domingo."

"You love them, eh?

"I guess," Liza started. "It seems that they showed up and everything got better. The day before we were wondering what would become of us. She leaned in and whispered. "I might have even been a little depressed. And now look. You're here." She hugged Katherine. "And Jimmy's home. And I'm going to be a grandma… AND we have llamas." Holding a braid in one hand, she turned, picking up the phone when it rang and whispered. "Do you want to talk to the doctor's office or want me to do it?"

"Go ahead. You know them."

Liza put the phone up to her ear. "Today at three? We can do that." She listened. "She doesn't have insurance, but she has us. We'll take care of it."

Katherine's eyes teared as Liza hung up the phone. "Thank you."

Liza finished the braid, then gave her a hug. "You're welcome." She glanced out of the window at the Jeep coming down the driveway. "Here's Freddy. Time to get this show on the road. Where's Henry and Jimmy?"

"In the barn, I think."

"Oh. "Liza smiled as the men greeted each other with handshakes. "You're all around the same age. Yesterday we were saying we could use help around here." The men came in as Liza pulled out a platter of bacon and scrambled eggs from the oven. "Morning, Freddy."

Holding hands as they settled around the table, Henry's voice filled with joy as he said the blessing.

"Mean looking Plymouth Fury you got there." Freddy drained his glass of orange juice. "Got a four block in it?"

"Yeah," Jimmy said. "She can move. Got a deal on her up in Canada."

Freddy studied Jimmy's face. Pot dealers in San Francisco drove cars like the Fury, for a quick getaway if needed.

Jimmy caught Freddy's stare, chuckled under his breath and shook his head. He met the vets eyes, expecting judgment, but instead saw amusement.

"I can take you two in the Jeep," Freddy said. "We'll follow Henry and Liza."

"Katherine has an appointment with the baby doctor at three, but we should be back long before then," Liza said.

Jimmy helped Katherine into the front seat, then hopped in back just as Abba's 'Dancing Queen' blasted through the speakers.

"Sorry." Freddy grinned over his shoulder at Jimmy, who was hanging over the seat. "I love the open country, but I like my music loud. ABBA's always blasting at our house. My folks are huge fans."

"Cool," Katherine said. "Where're you from?"

"Grew up in San Francisco," Freddy said. "Folks are lawyers… very involved in social causes. They live in a big yellow Victorian in the Haight. People always coming and going."

"What brought you to Oregon?" Jimmy asked.

"The llamas?" Freddy grinned in the rearview mirror as they passed the old willow with the broken swing.

"Whoa." Jimmy reached over to rest a hand on Katherine's shoulder. "That old swing finally gave out. Mom and Pop used to push us on it. Last time we were there, Pop, Chris and I carved our initials into that tree."

"Eh? I want to go see it sometime." Katherine said.

"We can fix it up for our kids."

"Kids?" Katherine chuckled.

"Just getting started, babe."

Freddy smiled to himself and eased the Jeep next to Henry and Liza's pickup. "Wait till you meet these two. They'll make you believe in magic."

The llamas ears perked at the sound of engines, watching with curious eyes as the vehicles rolled in.

Henry took the truck to a stop halfway up the hill and cut off the engine. "Just like Freddy said, stop short of the top. Think they'll come down?"

"Oh yes." Liza smiled as Freddy's car pulled up beside them and Katherine stepped out. "I can't wait for the kids to meet them." She opened the door and jumped out.

"Mom, with your braids and rolled-up overalls, you look like you're eighteen," Jimmy said, circling around the Jeep.

"That's why I married her." Henry gave Liza a squeeze. "Eternal youth."

Katherine turned her gaze up the hill as the llamas stood, still as statues, watching them. "Oh, Jimmy… look at them."

"Quick, Henry, lower the tailgate." Liza's voice trembled with excitement.

Freddy grabbed his bag and a couple of ropes from the back of the Jeep, tossing them into Henry's truck. "If we can catch 'em, I'd like to give them a quick checkup."

"I'll stay put," Katherine said leaning against the fender. "Doubt if I could get up there, eh?"

"Here they come." Henry gave Liza a boost into the truck bed, then leaned on the other side beside Katherine. Jimmy and Freddy slid into place between them.

"Apples and carrots are in the buckets behind us," Liza added.

"You okay, Katherine?" Henry whispered.

"Oh yes. I grew up in a small mountain community." She leaned over, smiling. "I'm used to this sort of thing."

Henry nodded as he took in this information. How could it be? Jimmy's home, and Katherine as close to perfect as he could imagine for a daughter-in-law. And a grandchild? Reaching down, he squeezed Liza's hand. She often told him that prayers are always answered, that one only needed to be patient.

Katherine's soft giggle was infectious as Domingo approached her. He sniffed her feet, then nosed his way into her maternity blouse, popping the button, exposing her belly. Soon, Liza started giggling and teased by the magic and excitement in the air, the whole group relaxed. Soft sounds and crunches were heard as the llamas nuzzled apples and carrots out of their hands.

Freddy reached behind them and pulled the rope around. He stretched an arm out and ran his fingers along the soft, downy fur of Bacardi's neck, careful not to touch his head and startle him. With his other hand he slipped the rope around the llama's neck, pulling it taut. "There ya go, fellow." He eased down off the tailgate. "Easy does it."

"Hand me a couple carrots." Freddy held his hand out and took them, leading Bacardi up the hill. Liza and Henry's heads were together, beaming at their success.

"Need your bag?" Henry called out.

"No, we'll save it for another day." He held the rope loose with one hand and held out a carrot with the other. Bacardi flattened his ears and raised his head as if to spit, then noticed the carrot. Freddy chuckled as the llama nudged it out of his hand. "Their curiosity gets the best of them." He looked over in surprise to see Jimmy had slipped the other rope around Domingo's neck while Liza held out an apple to him and smiled at the unfolding of the day.

"Great job, honey," Katherine called out.

Jimmy tried to follow Freddy's lead, but Domingo wasn't having it. At the tug of the rope, he flattened his ears and raised his head.

"Duck!" Freddy yelled as green spittle sprayed from Domingo's mouth, missing his target. Nostrils flaring, the llama glared at Jimmy as another mouthful of spittle erupted. Jimmy ducked and the spittle flew over the top of his head, landing square in Henry's face.

"Oh, God." Henry grabbed his handkerchief from his pocket and wiped off the green slime. "That stinks."

"Sorry, Dad." Jimmy looked up at Henry, a grin poking out of the side of his mouth as he tried not to laugh.

Jimmy tried to pull Domingo in close as the llama continued to struggle with the rope. Katherine came over, reached up, took Domingo's ears, and squeezed them tight, pulling the llama into her chest. "What are you doing?" Jimmy asked. "Be careful!"

"We had llamas on the farm, eh?" Katherine whispered to Domingo, releasing his ears as she ran a hand up and down his neck. "This is how we got them to settle down." Domingo took in a breath as if he was going to spit again, and then blew it out his nostrils, relaxing against Katherine as she let him nuzzle a carrot out of her hand.

"Okay," Freddy said. "That's enough for today but hold on to Domingo for a minute." He eased the rope off Bacardi and scratched his rump, calling out as the llama ran into the pasture. "You did good buddy."

Freddy covered Katherine's hands as she pulled away and ran his fingers up and down the llama's neck, then along his belly. "Everything looks healthy. Step away in case he spits again." Once clear, Freddy removed the rope and held out the last carrot. "Here ya go, Domingo," he whispered as the llama took the carrot, and stood watching him with a perplexed look, the carrot hanging out of his mouth.

"That went better than I expected." Freddy said. "Sorry Henry, but that sort of thing comes with the territory."

"I'll live," Henry said. "But I have first dibs on the shower."

Liza pinched her nose. "Jimmy can drive, and you can sit in the back."

"We'll work with the rope for a few more days." Freddy nodded to the llamas, who stood watching them. "I'd like to check their hooves and give them a deworming shot. No hurry."

"We better be getting back," Liza said. "Got a baby doctor to see."

Henry tossed Jimmy the keys and climbed into the bed of the pickup. "Been awhile since I rode back here." He settled down with his back to the cab. "Nice view."

Domingo and Bacardi stared as the vehicles drove away, perplexed by the day. This was all going to take some getting used to.

Little Sister Mountain Putucusi creaked with a low, ancient groan. "Growing pains."

King Llama's eyes sparkled with mischief. "Did you see that spit?" His chest swelled with pride. He turned toward the cliffside, where Chris sat, his feet hovering over the abyss, cradled by the whispering rustle of the trees. "Your body is merely an echo," King Llama spoke without sound, his words carried on currents of thought. "An illusion you left behind when you died."

Chris's form wavered, dissolving into a mist of rainbow light before solidifying again. "I know," he answered, his voice both near and far. "But it's how they recognize me. They're not ready to let go."

"It'll take time," whispered Little Sister Mountain Putucusi, her voice woven into the wind. She met King Llamas' gaze, their hearts beating a little faster with love for this man and his family.

Liza grinned at Jimmy. "I still can't believe it." He used one hand to steer the truck and took her hand with the other.

"I'm sorry I didn't call sooner, Mom. It must have been hard for you." They were quiet as they drove by the willow tree.

"Hey, take it easy in there," Henry called in through the cab window. "Almost bounced me out."

Liza smiled at her son. "Katherine tells me she wants to have her baby at home."

"Yeah, she grew up in a small commune. They raised their food, everything organic and natural."

"What would you think about fixing your old room up? It could be a nursery."

Jimmy hesitated.

"I mean," Liza frowned. "If you two want to stay."

"We don't want to be a problem for you and Pop. We haven't even discussed what happens next... wanted to get down here before the baby came."

"It's a big house." She gestured to the land. "And a lot of space. You're welcome for as long as you want to be here. Dad agrees."

"Thanks, mom."

"How about we hear what the doctor says, welcome this baby into the world, and then you and Katherine decide." A butterfly flew in circles off the side of the passenger window, catching Liza's attention. "So beautiful."

"What's that, Mom?"

"The butterfly. It's been flying around since we left the pasture."

"Maybe it's Chris whispering hello." He glanced at her out of the corner of his eyes as they made the final turn towards the house.

"That thought makes me happy. My heart says it's true." She reached over and touched his cheek. "Like I have both of my boys with me again."

ELEVEN

"Thanks," Katherine said with a grin as she stepped out of the bathroom. "At this rate, I should just set up camp in there. I wasn't sure my bladder was going to survive that bumpy ride back, eh?"

"No worries, young lady." Henry grabbed a towel from the hall closet and went into the bathroom.

The rest sat around the table as Liza put out cold bottles of soda pop and a bowl of pretzels. "You coming, Jimmy?"

"Yes, of course, Mom." He said. "Can't miss meeting the baby doctor. Back tomorrow, Freddy?"

"You bet."

"Come for breakfast. There'll be plenty." Liza said.

They waved as the Jeep drove past the barn and out of sight.

"He's a keeper, eh?" Katherine asked. "How did you find him?"

"Took over for the old vet. You remember Ken, right Jimmy? He retired about a year ago."

"Ah, better." Henry came out of the bathroom, draped in a red-striped terrycloth robe, wet hair slicked back. "Jimmy, why don't you pull the car out of the garage? We'll all fit."

"On it, pop." Jimmy grabbed the keys hanging on the hook near the back door, then turned, looking at them.

"Family affair." Liza said. "Such a wonderful feeling."

King Llama stood on the grassy expanse, poised between the ancient stone city and the jagged, time-forged steps that the Inca climbed for a thousand years. He gazed at Little Sister Mountain Putucusi, eyes softening as the breeze tousled the leaves on her trees, seeming to reach out in a hug, only to open, revealing her inner beauty.

Chris sat at the edge of the cave, his outline wavering in the light. He'd clung to the parts of himself he believed his loved ones would recognize, hoping to ease their passage into a future without him. He wanted them to know he would always be near. A feather's brush against a cheek, a butterfly dancing in circles around them… small, tender signs of his enduring love. In his days on the Earth plane, he had no idea of the enormity of the universe or the immensity of galaxies and stars. When the Starseeds sped past, tickling him with their energy, he remembered what a smile felt like on his face. Now, standing in the folds of this magical mountain, he turned his gaze to King Llama. Together, they cast a timeless smile into the universe, an offering of love to the world as they watched the clumsy, wonderstruck baby llamas, whose steps imprinted themselves upon the land and the hearts of its people.

The old doctor smiled at the shock in Katherine and Jimmy's eyes.

"Twins?" Shock filled their faces, followed by a burst of nervous laughter.

"Yes." Dr. Joe's blue eyes sparkled under bushy gray eyebrows, as they always did with the excitement of new parents. "And soon."

"Liza said it might be possible to give birth at home?" Katherine asked.

"It's been done." The doctor picked up the phone. "Martha around? Thanks, send her in."

The door opened and a slender woman with salt and pepper hair pulled back into a bun walked in. "I'm Martha, Dr. Joe's wife. I help with home births." At Martha's confident smile and kind eyes, Katherine's shoulders relaxed, as did the worry on her face.

"When the time nears, I'll come out daily and make sure everything is ready." She smiled at her husband. "When the baby is ready to come, we'll call Joe, and he'll come out to deliver."

"Babies," Dr. Joe said.

"Babies?" Martha opened and closed her mouth in surprise. "We're doing a home birth with twins?"

Jimmy's eyes grew wide. "Is that okay?"

Dr. McGrugor laughed. "Well, you tell me."

Jimmy blushed, making Katherine laugh. "So, home birth or not?" she asked.

"The babies are positioned well for an easy birth." Dr. Joe glanced at the frown on his wife's face and reached over, patting her hand. "If that stays the same, it should be fine."

"When do we think this will be happening?" Martha asked.

Dr. Joe looked at his notes, then up at the anticipation on everyone's faces. "A week? It's your first baby, so it might go slow, might go fast." The phone jingled on Dr. Joe's desk. Picking it up, he nodded. "Be right there." He stood. "Martha will arrange everything with you. I have a baby to deliver."

On the drive home, the car was initially filled with stunned silence, the energy like a bubble ready to burst. Henry stopped at the only light in town, cranked down the window, and let out a bellow, followed by: "We're having twins!" People on the street smiled and waved.

Liza reached over, to stop him from embarrassing them, but then a light went off on her face. "You're dag gone right! Henry! We're having twins!" Jimmy and Katherine huddled in the back seat, giggling.

"Woo Hoo!" Henry honked his horn and yelled at the folks on the next block. "We're having twins!" Driving by the old Standard station, he slowed down as old Max hung up the nozzle on the pump. "Twins, Max! We're having twins! And we have llamas!"

Max looked up in puzzled surprise, then a broad grin broke out. It didn't matter if what Henry said made any sense or not. He hadn't seen his friend this happy in years. "Congratulations!" he yelled as they sped off. On the country road back to the house, the stunned silence became busy chatter.

"Your and Chris's room," Liza turned to Jimmy. "It'll be perfect for a nursery." Her eyes grew misty. "The old cradles are out in the shed. Might still be useable."

Katherine nestled into Jimmy's arms, unsure whether to cry or laugh. Things were happening so fast.

"Baby clothes." Henry mused. "Did you keep their old clothes?"

"Of course I did Henry." Liza said. "But the moths might have gotten them by now. We need to go shopping!"

"Martha said she'd be out tomorrow at eleven," Katherine said.

Henry glanced over his shoulder, winking at Jimmy. "We got a busy afternoon ahead of us."

TWELVE

King Llama's heart swelled with joy, filling him with pride at the unfolding of new beginnings in the world. He looked over the gorge to Little Sister Mountain Putucusi. Chris stood at the edge, dressed in army fatigues, tears sparkling like raindrops.

Powerless to stop it, Chris had watched sadness settle over his parents and witnessed his brother's quiet struggle to make peace with the choices he'd made. Yet he'd also seen the first signs of healing as Jimmy slowly opened his heart to love. Longing to reach out, to let them know he was still with them in spirit, even if not in body, Chris's yearning rose into the air in soft tendrils of pink and green. He materialized beside King Llama on the grassy plaza, his human form a tapestry of light and shadow, an ephemeral dance of energy that bursts forth like sparklers igniting the midnight sky.

"Sparklers," Chris said. "They were my favorite thing on the fourth of July. We wrote our names in the air and wove circles around each other."

With long, thick lashes framing his ancient eyes, King Llama met Chris's gaze. "Soon, there will be new life born right in the bedroom you grew up in. The journey is ongoing in this infinite universe, and the time is nearing for me to join the stars and our ancestors on the mountaintops."

Claud stood by the open patio door, watching the sunlight dance across the ocean, scattering rainbows in every direction. Just last night, she had stood on the balcony, mesmerized as the sea faded to a soft, shimmering gray. Her eyes drifted upward as the first star blinked to life above the nearly full moon.

Grief had lingered long into the night. But this morning, the tears streaming down her cheeks were tears of joy. Was it the memory of him? The gift of having known such love? She wasn't sure. She shrugged gently and looked down at the envelope in her hands. Running her fingers over the address, she breathed in, steady and sure. She knew what she needed to do.

THIRTEEN

High in the mountains of Peru, a butterfly perched on King Llama's nose, its silken hues of violet and sapphire dancing with the breath of the wind. King Llama twitched his ears and wrinkled his nose, but the tiny spirit paid no mind as it reveled in the wonder of its first flight, its first touch of the world beyond the cocoon. King Llama was sure he could hear Little Sister Mountain Putucusi's giggle at the playfulness of this new spirit. The butterfly lifted off King Llama's nose and flew into the breeze, delighted at the freedom of gliding on the air waves.

Liza sneezed, waving away the dust filled air. It took them two hours to make their way through everything in the shed to the corner filled with boxes of baby memorabilia, which were nestled in between the two cradles.

"Good thing you keep everything, Liza." The sarcasm in his voice belied the grin on his face.

"Never know when you'll need it." She sneezed again. They pulled the boxes and cradles out into the waning sunlight.

"Cradles are in decent shape," Henry said, standing them up next to each other. "Need new mattresses, though. That should be easy enough."

"Glad I packed everything well." Liza pulled heavy plastic bags out of the box, opening one. "Look, Henry. These are the blankets we wrapped Chris and Jimmy in when we brought them home from the hospital." She hugged them to her chest. "They're like brand new."

"We'll have to go into Portland to find mattresses, but these frames will clean up just fine." He wiped his face with his handkerchief. "The cribs are here somewhere. But we won't need them for a while."

"Let's go check on the kids," Liza said.

Katherine sat on the bed as Jimmy boxed up the last of the clothing in the closet.

"I'm keeping our letter jackets out for now. Not sure why." He held up his jacket for her to see.

"Tell me about your days on the football team, eh, Jimmy?"

"Chris was the quintessential star quarterback, the do-no-wrong golden boy." Jimmy brushed the corners of the closet with the broom, knocking out old cobwebs, then stepped out, leaning the broom into the corner. "Clean cut, followed the rules, or so he made everyone believe." Chuckling, he came over and sat next to Katherine. "The shenanigans we pulled… I got credit for most of them."

Katherine pulled her legs out and stretched them into Jimmy's lap. He pulled her socks off and began massaging her feet. She groaned. "Did you resent him for that?"

"Is this your sneaky way of scoring a foot rub?"

"Is it working?" She smiled, eyes heavy. "You're ignoring my question, but that's okay. Keep rubbing. What position did you play?"

"Wide receiver. Somewhere around here there's a scrapbook with a picture of me from the newspaper, catching the ball in the end zone." He dropped her feet, demonstrating the play. "Spectacular."

"Feet, Jimmy. Pay attention."

"Oh, sorry."

"Tell me about the shenanigans."

Working the bottoms of her feet, he laughed. "One summer, I think we were sixteen, we were driving up and down Main Street. Bored, mainly. The light turned green, but we sat blocking traffic, talking to some cute girls."

"Didn't you have a girlfriend?"

"Nah, nothing serious. We had fun, but football and the farm were our life."

"Ouch. Lighter, eh?"

He stopped and held her feet cradled in his hands. "Remember Old Max at the gas station?"

"Mmmm hmm."

"His brother, Donald, was the local cop. All bluster and no brine." He chuckled at the memory. "He yelled and chased us off from flirting with those girls."

"And then?"

"About an hour later, still cruising, we saw him parked under a tree, his hiding place, eating a sandwich. We also knew that after eating, he would fall asleep."

"Hmmm…" Katherine's eyelids drooped.

"It was Chris's idea. We parked about a half block away, and Chris got leftover firecrackers from the fourth of July out of the trunk, then snuck over, lit one, and threw it under Donald's squad car."

"You were the getaway driver, eh?"

Jimmy laughed. "Yep, he jumped in, and we sped off, not looking back after the loud bang. Never got caught. But I guarantee you, if we had, I would have gotten the blame." Sighing, he leaned his head against the wall, closing his eyes, breathing in the comforts of home.

Waking from her light sleep, Katherine reached out and covered his hand with hers.

"Resent him?

"No, we understood each other."

Henry and Liza peeked around the bedroom door at the sleeping couple. Nodding towards the kitchen, she whispered. "Let's make dinner."

Claud hung up the old black desk phone, letting her hand rest on it for a moment, listening as the sound of crashing waves announced the incoming tide. Her landlord was cool about her breaking the lease early. With news of soldiers returning from the war being spit on, his support had come as a surprise. Somehow, she slipped into the country after Vietnam and found a place to lie low and heal. Even though the furnishings in her apartment were simple and sparse, she felt safe here, and was finally able to sleep a full eight hours without nightmares. She would miss the walks on the beach, as well as the dog she'd planned to adopt over the summer. But the landlord was understanding and told her she was welcome back anytime.

So, if things don't work out…

Sounds of laughter came from the farmhouse kitchen as the foursome sat around the table, each with an empty bowl, once filled with chili sprinkled with cubes Velveeta cheese. In the middle of the table sat a plate with a solitary piece of cornbread surrounded by crumbs. Liza opened the refrigerator and took out a gallon of strawberry ice cream. "Henry, help me dish this out." Soon, he stood at her side, getting bowls out of the cupboard, scooper in hand.

"What about that song you told me about earlier, eh?" Katherine asked. "Something about a hole in the bucket?" Jimmy groaned.

Henry snapped the towel in Liza's direction, who shook her head as he sang:

"There's a hole in the bucket, dear Liza, dear Liza.
There's a hole in the bucket, dear Liza, a hole."

Liza did a little bow and curtsy, grinning at Jimmy and Katherine.

"So fix it, dear Henry, dear Henry, dear Henry.
So fix it, dear Henry, dear Henry, fix it."

Henry cleared his throat and leaned in.

"With what should I fix it, dear Liza, dear Liza?
With what should I fix it dear Liza with what?

"With a stick dear Henry, dear Henry, dear Henry.
With a stick, dear Henry, dear Henry a stick."

Several verses later…

"But Liza? With what should I fetch it, dear Liza,
dear Liza?
With what should I fetch it, dear Liza? With what?"

"In the bucket dear Henry…"

"But there's a hole in the bucket…"

The couple bowed while Katherine, grinning ear to ear, clapped. "I love it! What made you start singing it?"

Henry smiled. "I grew up listening to my grandparents, and then my parents, sing it, only they sang it in German.

**"Ein Loch ist im Eimer, oh Liza, Oh Liza.
Ein Loch ist im Eimer, oh Liza, Ein Loch."**

"Oh, not again." Jimmy put his hands over his ears.

"One day, Katherine, when we have a more appreciative audience…" Henry stuck his tongue out at Jimmy. "We'll sing the whole thing in German for you."

"How fun, I can't wait." She poked Jimmy in the ribs with her elbow and asked Henry. "But why this song?

"Oh, I don't know." Henry set bowls of ice cream down on the table while Liza poured tea. "Perhaps it's a reminder not to let life, going in circles as it always does, get you down." He shrugged. "History repeats itself over and over, and do humans learn? Not really. So, we write fun jingles that remind us to laugh and not take everything so seriously."

"They used to run around the house in the morning, singing it while Chris and I got ready for school," Jimmy said.

"And you know what?" Liza asked.

"There's still a hole in the bucket… right outside the barn." Henry laughed.

As evening wound down, yawns began to interrupt the conversation. "Martha's coming by around eleven tomorrow, so we can get the nursery set up. Is Freddy coming too?" Katherine asked.

"Yes, in the morning," said Liza. "It won't take long to move the furniture into the nursery. Jimmy and Henry can go out with Freddy to check on the llamas while you're meeting with Martha."

"Perfect." Katherine said.

"Night, Dad and Mom." Jimmy took Katherine's hand. "Thank you for everything."

"It means so much to have you home." Liza said. "I still can't believe you're here."

"Believe it." Jimmy winked.

Standing on the ancient terraces of Machu Picchu, Chris felt the rhythm and vibrations of his parents old song reverberate through the air. His heart sang along like moonbeams dancing in the sky, remembering a happy childhood, soft grass under his feet as he ran, and later cleats on the football field, sounds of cheering from the bleachers when they made a touchdown. His parents were always in the stands, guardians of his earliest dreams

King Llama lifted his gaze as the first star of the night appeared above Little Sister Mountain Putucusi. In that moment, the tapestry of fate wove itself from luminous threads, and with each spark, a collective smile swept up into the stars, the same stars Domingo and Bacardi watched from the faraway Oregon pasture. Bellies full and spirits content, their souls, though not yet understanding the full measure of their sacred mission, nestled into the earth's gentle embrace, surrendering to the quiet magic of night.

FOURTEEN

Liza leaned against the kitchen counter, adding to the list of items needed for the birthing. "Good morning," she said to Henry's footsteps.

"You're up with the chickens this morning." Henry poured coffee into his mug, then opened the fridge for cream. "Oh, that's right… We don't have any."

"Chickens, yes…" Liza scratched an item off the list and scribbled in another. "With more mouths to feed, chickens are a good idea. Think the old coop is still usable?"

"Coffee first. What's on the list?"

"Things Martha wants on hand for the birthing, mattresses for the cradles, curtains for the nursery…" She waved her hand and read the list again, scratching her head. "I planned to sew new curtains, but with everything going on, there's no time."

"I'm surprised you don't have curtains stashed away somewhere."

"I'll look in the linen chest. And a bedspread to match." She refilled her cup and sat with Henry at the table. "I thought we could put one of the twin beds in the shed and leave the other one in case Martha needs to stay over."

"That works," Henry nodded.

"Freddy called earlier, had an emergency at the clinic. He'll be out this afternoon," Liza said.

"Thought I heard the phone ring," Henry said. "Me and Jimmy can go check on the llamas. We'll measure out space for a shelter." He got up and stared out the window. "Thought it might rain today, but all I see is blue sky and sun. What time is Martha coming?"

"Eleven," a voice said from the bottom of the stairs.

"Good morning, Katherine." Liza reached up and got two more mugs from the cupboard. "Sleep well?"

"Yes. It's very peaceful here."

"I'm so glad. Have a seat, breakfast is about ready." Liza glanced over as Jimmy came into the kitchen. "Good Lord, son, your hair's almost down to your waist."

"Muller genes." He laughed and poured the last of the coffee. "I'll make another pot."

Liza set a platter of scrambled eggs and bacon in the center of the table. "Toast coming up. Making coffee, Jimmy?"

"Yep, percolating away."

Henry poured orange juice into the small glasses saved from pimiento cheese jars and held his glass up in a toast. "An official welcome to Katherine. I can't imagine a more wonderful gift my son could have brought us."

"Cheers," everyone called out.

Katherine blushed. "Thank-you. I couldn't have imagined anything better." She snuggled her head into Jimmy's hug.

"You're welcome here as long as you want to stay," Henry started. "This morning, Liza suggested chickens. Now, with the llamas, what's to stop us from getting a couple of goats and sheep?"

"And a cow for cream." Liza turned to Jimmy and Katherine. "We don't want to assume. You two might have other plans."

"Thanks." Jimmy took Katherine's hand. "We'd love to get our feet on the ground and get these babies born." He shook his head. "Babies. I worried about managing one."

"Speaking of," Henry said, rising to his feet. "Help me take one of the beds out of your old room. Then we can set up the nursery."

Soon, sounds of shuffling furniture came from the bedroom above them, followed by Jimmy sliding the mattress down the stairs, humping it out the back door. Two more trips saw bed slats, frame, and headboard go by. Shortly, Henry poked his head in from outdoors. "We're off to check on the llamas."

"Give them a smooch for me," Liza said as the door swung shut. "Do you watch TV?" Liza asked Katherine. "Mary Tyler Moore is on tonight."

"We didn't have a TV where we lived. What's it about?"

"It's a comedy about a single woman and her life in the city. It's fun. That Betty White is a spitfire. But the final episode is tonight. Then Henry will want to see Bonanza."

"It's a date. Betty White, isn't that the actress who supports animal causes?" Katherine asked.

"Yes." Liza cleared the dishes from the table. "She's sort of a mean girl on the show, but in real life, she's kind and is an advocate for animals."

"Can't wait." Katherine stood. "Here, let me help you with those dishes, eh?"

"You never mind," Liza said. "I'm sure your feet ache. Trust me, you have plenty of dishes coming your way. Sit and chat with me. More coffee?"

"Sure, thanks." Katherine sat back down.

"How do you feel about having two babies?" Liza asked, filling Katherine's cup and setting the cream next to it.

"Both excited and nervous." Katherine twirled hair around her finger. "Better now that we're here. I wonder if we should keep the cradles in our room or if it would be better to start them out in their own room?"

"Henry and I kept our babies close so we would hear them if they woke." Liza cleared dishes off the table. "But as they grew, the room got too small for all of us, so we went from cradles to cribs and eventually twin beds in their room."

"Did you have to discipline them much?"

"You mean spare the rod, spoil the child type of thinking?"

"No, you don't seem like that. Where I grew up, with my parents dying when I was young, we were left to figure it out. We had good and bad days but always helped each other. Wasn't much fighting. Not much to fight over. If we wanted to eat, we had to tend the animals and garden, so we were outside a lot."

"Well, you're a lovely young woman. I couldn't have wished for a better or prettier daughter-in-law."

Katherine blushed and held her belly. "Ah, they're doing somersaults. Want to feel?"

Liza's eyes brightened as she reached over and touched Katherine's pregnant belly. A lump the size of a tennis ball pushed out. "Ohhhh… this is happening, isn't it?"

"Yes," Katherine beamed. "It is." Liza glanced at the clock. "Martha will be here soon. Let's check out the nursery, and we can raid the linen chest for curtains."

Liza rinsed the last dish and put it on the rack.

Henry and Jimmy rolled over the lower pasture, reflective in their thoughts.

"Heavy rain last year, creeks high." Henry slowed as they neared the willow.

"Stop the truck, Dad. Let's visit." Henry pulled over and turned off the engine. Katherine wanted to stop here yesterday, but I wasn't ready." Jimmy sighed, looking over at his father. "Still taking it all in, I guess."

The men walked toward the old tree, happy for the shade. Jimmy pulled on the remaining rope where the swing used to hang. "Gave up the ghost, huh?"

"Now, there's a story," Henry told him about the llamas and Liza's dress, followed by the near disaster on the swing. "I'm tired of playing it safe, she said. Push higher, I want to feel my boys, she said." Pausing, he put his hand on Jimmy's shoulder. "Llamas springing up like magic, you come home with a pregnant wife. All because my wife decided she's tired of playing it safe?" Tears filled Henry's eyes. "We have joy in our lives again, Jimmy. It's like angels in heaven rained down gifts into our life. I thought the light had gone out of your mom's eyes forever." He pulled the handkerchief out of his pocket and blew his nose. "Yeah, son, life can change on a dime. And this time, the coin flipped heads up."

Jimmy walked over to the tree and traced his fingers over their initials. "A lot has happened since we carved these."

"What happened? Why didn't you write?"

"To be honest, I don't know. Once I got over the border, I went up into the mountains to a small community where a lot of draft dodgers went. I got into the drug scene for a while, but it didn't agree with me. Too many years playing football. I didn't like the way it made my body feel, or my mind."

"Thank God for football."

Tracing his fingers over Chris's initials, Jimmy said. "Always the golden boy, followed the rules… at least that's what you thought. Up north, it felt like a piece of me had been cut out. I'd never been away from him for even a day. But I couldn't do the Army, Vietnam, and all that." He sat down heavily on a nearby rock. "Took time to figure it out. I wrote once, but then everyone said the government was watching the mail. Probably baloney, but I didn't want to cause trouble for you."

"Scoot over," Henry said, sitting beside his son. "Let's get one thing straight. Chris didn't fool anyone. Remember that firecracker stunt under Sheriff Don's car?"

"How did you know about that?"

"The day after, the Sheriff paid us a visit. Someone saw Chris throw the firecracker under the car and run away."

Jimmy stared at his father, wide-eyed.

Henry shook his head. "Liza and I always wondered what lay behind the, what did you call it, the golden boy mask? It was almost a relief that he went into the Army, if only for the rules and structure he needed. But we sure didn't get the outcome we hoped for."

"Dad…." Jimmy sat in silence, searching for words.

"We always knew what you were about. You're authentic and always made your opinions clear, appropriate or not." Henry chuckled. "But I always believed you. We felt better when you two were together."

"Geez, how could I have gotten it so wrong? I spent years up in Canada, feeling guilty for how I turned out."

"We loved both of you. The gift of being a father to you and Chris, I wouldn't give that up for anything. You know what's odd, Jimmy?"

"What's that?"

"These llamas, one black and one white, mirrors of each other are sort of like you and Chris. Somehow, it seems like a part of God's grand plan. Perhaps that's what faith is all about. Perhaps the llamas came to remind us that we still have a bit of life in these old bones. And joy."

Jimmy got up and walked over to the creek where he knelt and splashed water over his face before taking a drink. He sat up and gazed at the fast-running water. "You have no idea, Pop, of how many times I lay in bed, thinking about this creek. Whenever my life felt like it was spinning out of control, I closed my eyes and remembered this, the steady flow, the ripples." He gestured towards the water. "Always calmed me down."

Henry stood and leaned against the tree. "A fine woman you got, Jimmy. How did you meet?"

"I was doing my thing up on the mountain, and one day I heard a truck coming up, but it stopped short of the driveway."

"Wait a minute. Explain doing your thing."

"Oh, all right, since you already know everything. A bunch of us were growing pot, and we were a little paranoid about who came up the road. Well, a lot paranoid actually. Sometimes, the authorities looked the other way, other times, they didn't. But paranoia became a way of life. So, the day I heard the truck, I grabbed my shotgun, snuck down the hillside, and hid behind the trees." He chuckled. "And there she stood. You should've seen her, kicking the flat tire, hands on her hips, furious at the world. Katherine was delivering a load of vegetables to someone farther up the mountain and wasn't in the mood for a flat tire."

"She's got a strong spirit."

"You ain't seen nothing yet." Jimmy laughed out loud. "Love at first sight for me. I changed her tire and sent her on her way but couldn't quit thinking about her." He joined his father. "A week or so later, I took my share of the profits and walked away. Found her at that commune she lived in. Never looked back."

"She knows about the pot business?"

"I don't think she'd be surprised, but I never told her. I also didn't tell her about the wad of cash I have. I made a lot of money."

"One thing Liza and I discovered that got us through life together was being honest with each other. There needs to be one person in your life who you can be transparent with, no matter the cost. Liza and I chose each other. I have a hunch your Katherine might understand."

"You might be right." Jimmy's face filled with surprise. "Well, I'll be doggoned. Lookie there." Peering over the bed of the pickup were Domingo and Bacardi, ears perked up as they stared at the men, round eyes full of curiosity.

"Well, well, well…" Henry whispered. He reached over the side, pulling out the bag of apples and carrots, while Jimmy got the rope. "Hey fellas." He held out an apple in one hand and a carrot in the other. The llamas glanced at each other and took a step forward, but then, at the sound of Freddy's truck, ran back up the hill.

Freddy jumped out. "Hey, making progress! You'll have them down in the barn in no time."

Henry pulled down the tailgate and hopped up. "Mark my words. They'll come back." He took a bite out of a carrot. "These are tasty. I can see why they like 'em."

FIFTEEN

Claud gripped the steering wheel as she muscled through LA traffic, chastising herself for not timing things better. She got off the freeway and took Route 66. Slower, but better than sitting in bumper-to-bumper traffic, inching along. The Eagles blared Hotel California on the radio. Humming along, she turned up the radio as Dancing Queen came on. "Love me some Abba." She pulled into a drive-in for lunch and a chance to look at the map. "Maybe I should find a place along here for the night." But after a burger and a shake, she decided to press on. Only an hour to Bakersfield, and her mom. She hadn't seen her since getting back from Vietnam. Pulling hair away from her hot, sweaty face, Claud wrapped it into a bun as she pondered what to do. I could stay a couple of days… or not. She'd stop at the next phone booth along the way and call, check the mood of the day. Relieved to see the ladies room near the entrance of the building, she headed inside. After the cramped ride in her little Fold Pinto, it felt good to stretch her legs.

Jimmy joined Henry on the tailgate while Freddy leaned against the side of the truck, rope in hand, ready for action. Bacardi and Domingo hung back at first, observing, but curiosity soon got the best of them, and they wandered back to the truck.

Domingo stepped forward, pausing to glance back at his brother. Bacardi snorted. Domingo shot him a glare, then turned and approached the truck, taking a carrot from Henry's hand. Soon, Bacardi, encouraged by his brother's bravery, ambled over to join them.

Freddy slipped the rope over Bacardi's nose and snugged it around his neck. "Good job, Bacardi. Hey Jimmy, bring a couple of carrots over here." Jimmy jumped down. "Now, take the rope and pull him in close. That's it."

"Hold tight." But Bacardi wasn't having it. Jimmy squeezed the llama's ears, just as Katherine had shown him, pulling Bacardi closer to his chest until he began to calm down. Freddy lifted each leg in turn, examining his hooves.

"Neat and trim. You are a young one," Freddy said, running his hands down the llama's back and along his underbelly."

Freddy took the rope off Bacardi and looked over at Domingo. "Want to go next, fella?"

The two women stood arm in arm, as Martha's old, red Studebaker pulled up. "I'm nervous," Katherine said.

"Me too," Liza whispered, putting an arm on her daughter-in-law's shoulder. "Remember, we got this. No worries about cost. We have babies to welcome. Oh, I can't wait to hold them."

Martha waved hello and got her brown, paisley medical bag out of the back. Once inside, Liza gave her a tour. Katherine lagged as the trio went up the stairs.

"That's quite a trek for you." Martha's voice was kind, but Liza saw a concerned look on the nurse's face as she led them into Jimmy and Katherine's room.

"I wondered about that," Liza said. "No reason Henry and I couldn't swap rooms with you guys for a little while."

"Let's make this work." Katherine leaned against the door jam, catching her breath. "I like it up here." She went over and opened the curtains, allowing the sun to shine in.

"Lucky you, there's a bathroom up here," Martha said. "This is perfect if you don't mind the stairs."

"The nursery is across the hall from our room."

"Where do you want to do the birthing?" Martha asked.

"We thought we might put the cradles in our room at first," Katherine said. "Will that work?"

"Sure." Martha glanced around. "There's plenty of room for everything."

A hint of relief softened Katherine's face. "How is this possible?" She hugged Liza. "Thank you."

Liza beamed. "Henry and I will go into Portland this afternoon and buy the things on the list." She stood with her back to them as Martha helped Katherine lie on the bed and examined her.

"Sounds like you have healthy babies in here. Doing somersaults?" Martha laughed. "You're about one and a half centimeters dilated, so it's moving along. "I'll call you in the morning and see how you're doing. If your water breaks or you start having contractions, call me, day or night."

"Any idea of how long?" Katherine asked.

"When your water breaks or you're dilated to five, I'll stay here until they come. And when your dilated to eight, we'll call Joe." Martha squeezed her hand. "Babies have their own timing, but if you keep going at this rate, we're probably looking at next week, or sooner."

A shiver ran down Katherine's spine as she ran her hands over her belly. "I can't believe it."

"For now, eat and drink as usual." Martha smiled at Liza. "And plenty of foot and back rubs. A hot bath is soothing if someone can help you."

"Jimmy will," Katherine said.

Martha waved to the men on her way out of the driveway.

"Everything okay?" Henry asked.

"Yes, but we should go into Portland today," Liza said. "I'll feel better when everything is set up. I think these babies are in a hurry to be born."

"How are the llamas?" Katherine asked.

"Jimmy and I stopped at the willow tree, and they came down to the truck," Henry said. "Surprised the heck out of us."

"Wish I'd been there. They're cool, eh?" Katherine gazed out at the pasture beyond the barn, a quiet longing in her eyes. "They remind me to be happy. And to laugh."

"How about you and Jimmy hold down the fort while Liza and I tackle that shopping list?" Henry asked.

"What do ya say? Jimmy asked. "Think we can handle it?"

"For sure." Katherine laughed. "I'll keep him in line, eh?"

"Let me show you the linen chest," Lisa said. "See if you can find curtains and a bedspread for the nursery. We'll call you from the diner to see if you found anything you like."

"Diner?" Jimmy raised his eyebrows.

"Yep." Henry put his arm around Liza. "I'm taking my honey on a date after we do the shopping. There's a new diner in town."

Freddy stood back, enjoying the camaraderie.

Henry grinned at the vet. "Let me walk you out."

At the slam of the door, Henry spoke. "We appreciate you coming out and giving us a hand. Send me the bill?"

Freddy smiled. "It's fun. Who would have thought llamas would show up out of the blue? Think of the stories you'll have to tell your grandchildren. I hear it's gonna be twins."

"Yep. Who would have thought it?" Henry clapped him on the back. "Hey Freddy, I know your parents are up north. You're welcome to stop by anytime. Consider yourself family."

"Thanks, Henry. I might take you up on that."

Liza came out of the house, a black leather purse hanging over her arm. "Ready?" Henry called out.

"Ready as I'll ever be." Liza's dress swirled around her calves as she came down the steps.

"Got the list?" Henry asked.

She waved it in the air. "See you tomorrow, Freddy?"

"I have surgery in the morning, but I'll be out in the afternoon."

"Look forward to it. See ya tomorrow."

Jimmy and Katherine stood at the kitchen window watching the cars fade in the distance.

"Your parents are so lovely," Katherine said.

"They've always been decent people, and I've put them through a lot. My dad asked why I hadn't written."

"Why didn't you?"

"I don't know. I blamed it on the government, but really, I couldn't think of anything to write. Thought they'd be disappointed in me."

"It appears they're anything but."

"Katherine, come here." He took her hand and headed up the stairs to their room.

"Slow down, Buster. You've got a baby train behind you, eh?"

"Sorry." In their room, he patted the bed. "Sit down, I want to talk." Jimmy pulled out his pack, dug into the bottom, and pulled out a wad of Canadian dollars, undid the rubber band, and laid it on the bed.

Katherine whistled, picking it up. "What in the world? Where did this come from?"

"I talked to Pop this morning. He advised me to be honest with you."

"What did you do, rob a bank?"

"No. Before I met you, I grew weed up on the mountain."

"Oh, you were one of them? Everyone knows about that place. Guess I'm lucky you didn't shoot me when my tire went flat, eh?"

"Shoot you?" He took her shoulders, turning her to face him. "You standing there, swearing and waving your arms in the air, kicking the tire. It was love at first sight for me." He chuckled and ran his fingers over her cheek. "As soon as possible, I settled with my partners, took my share of the profits, and left. Best decision I've ever made."

"Jimmy, there's enough here to... buy a house, pay for the babies..."

"I know, I told my dad, but he said not to worry. He said honesty and transparency is what kept their marriage strong over the years. Suggested I do the same."

Her eyes narrowed. "So that bit about you helping out on a farm? Nonsense?"

"Not really, I just didn't say what kind of farm."

"I should have known," she said, eyebrows raised. "What now, Jimmy? Are you going to keep breaking the law? I don't want a jailbird for a husband."

"No, I want a better life for us. I met you and walked away from it. We can stay here or go somewhere else. But I wanted to tell you everything, and I wanted you to know that moneywise, we're okay."

She leaned in and put her forehead against his. "Promise me one thing, Jimmy."

"Anything."

"Never lie to me again."

"Okay."

"No, I want to hear the words come out of your mouth and see in your eyes that you mean it." She held his gaze, her brown eyes steady. "I've had a lot of liars in my life. I need to know I can trust you."

He cupped her chin with his hand and spoke. "I promise you, Katherine Muller. I will never lie to you again."

"Okay." She snuggled into his arms. "I love you, Jimmy. So much."

"You have no idea." Jimmy hugged her and kissed the top of her head. "Dreams are coming true that I didn't even know I had."

Jimmy pulled away and caressed her cheek. "Let's go see the llamas."

SIXTEEN

King Llama lazed on the grassy plaza, basking in the warmth of the sun. Visitors milled around him, stopping with cameras ready, unaware they carried away more than a picture. The ancient energy of the sacred city, woven into terraces, stones, and the very breath of the mountains, would imprint itself on them, whispering its quiet power into their lives forever. The legacy of the Inca still pulsed, undiminished by time.

To his left, Huayna Picchu, the mother of this city, stretched her spiraling peaks toward the sky. Veiled in the last traces of morning mist, she revealed hidden hollows, her quiet strength radiating through the valley. To his right, the great guardian, Machu Picchu Mountain, stood steadfast, safeguarding the ancient stone city. At dawn, dedicated seekers scaled its heights, yearning to see the sunrise as the Inca had, drawn by an unspoken call echoing through the centuries. A group now descended from the Sun Gate, their voices alight with wonder of an energy that transcended words, a knowing beyond thought.

King Llama flicked an ear, gazing at Little Sister Mountain Putucusi. Nestled between the mother and father mountains, her presence was the quiet keeper of balance. Sweetness and strength intertwined within and around her, as in all things that endured.

An older woman limped into the plaza, her shoulders heavy with quiet sorrow. "I can't make the climb," she confessed to the guide, her voice edged with regret. The dream of standing atop

Huayna Picchu, touching the sky from its heights, had slipped beyond her grasp. Instead, the guide led her to a sunlit grass expanse overlooking the gorge. She thanked her softly and sat, surrendering to disappointment, until she lifted her gaze. Across the gorge, Putucusi opened her arms ever so slightly.

King Llama watched as the woman held her face up to the sun's warmth, receiving the love from Little Sister, always present, always in perfect balance of all that is. A small lizard scrambled up the side of the rock, pausing as a sparrow flitted down to join them, tilting its head in gentle acknowledgement.

The woman glanced at them, smiling in welcome, and together they sat in quiet communion. As the lizard and swallow looked on, she lay back on the grass while the mountain's unseen waves of healing rippled outward, dissolving thoughts of not being strong enough, good enough, or just enough, of anything. The wind carried those doubts away, leaving behind only the knowledge that while there would always be layers and challenges, she was enough. Of whatever. Always.

King Llama closed his eyes, feeling the shift of ancient harmony restoring itself. He gazed at Putucusi with deep gratitude, his heart swelling as he saw the silent, sacred exchange between the mountain and the woman. Perhaps, one day, she would welcome a llama into her life, a quiet companion carrying the wisdom and endurance of his kind. And perhaps, little by little, she would share with the world the secret known to the Inca, the llamas, and the mountains themselves: Some healings cannot be spoken. They can only be felt.

"Ah, Mom." Jimmy fumbled with his coffee cup, then stood and put it in the sink. "Church? Really?"

"Words gotten around that you're back." Liza looked at him with hopeful eyes. "Everyone wants to see you and meet Katherine."

"I'd kind of like to go, eh?" Katherine said.

"What about the babies?" Jimmy started. "What if you go into labor at church?"

"Now that would be the talk of the town." Henry chuckled. "Make the fake flowers on Helen's hat crumble and fall off."

"Henry," Liza scolded and turned to Katherine. "Helen is the local naysayer. She has a narrow view of right and wrong and doesn't mind telling you."

"You can say that again," Henry said.

"Life hasn't been very kind to her," Liza continued. "Yet somehow, in her own way, she shows up and does what she can."

"Interesting," Katherine said. "Why do you describe her as a naysayer?"

"Her father was a preacher in the next town over. Both parents were very strict, prim and proper, you might say. She ran off with her high school sweetheart, got married and settled here. Johnny, her husband, worked for the local tractor supply."

"Bought that old Harvester from him," Henry said.

"They tried and tried, but she couldn't get pregnant. Johnny took to drinking, and one night crossed the double line into an oncoming semi."

"That's awful," Katherine said.

"Helen became bitter over time. I guess you could say she became her parents. She put all her energy into the church. While quick with an opinion, she still organizes community potlucks after the service. When Chris died and Jimmy left, she called every other day, filling me in on all the local gossip, or her version of it. I got tired of it, but it kept me talking. She brought us food, made sure we were okay."

"She never married again?"

"No," Liza said. "She's an attractive woman, and men have tried."

"Max has been sweet on her for years," Henry said. "But she's cold as ice. Poor guy, doesn't give up."

"Bitterness gets in the way," Liza said. "No one judges her more than she judges herself. But she gets under Henry's skin."

"Let's do it, Jimmy," Katherine said. "I'm feeling good and would love to get out. Once the babies come, it might be a while before we have another chance, eh?"

Liza covered the tuna casserole with tin foil and put it in a shopping bag. "There's a potluck after the service, so maybe we can talk to that couple with the llamas next county over."

"Not sure I'm ready for this, but I guess we're going," Jimmy said.

Katherine kissed his cheek. "I'll change my clothes."

Jimmy watched Katherine begin her trek up the stairs and then leaned into his dad.

"Will I be accepted back?"

"By now, word has spread that you're home, so no one will be surprised. You might get a look or two, but that's all. Stick with me, we'll manage." Henry grinned. "And I doubt anyone could resist the charm of that wife of yours."

A fly buzzed around Domingo, twitching his ears. His stomach rumbled, like a spit starting up, but when the fly darted off, he realized it was just hunger. Restless, he wandered the tree line, marveling at the sweetness of the tall grass. Bacardi lay nearby, watching his brother's antics. In his young world, he found it better to sit back and wait. The right action always seemed to become clear at exactly the right time.

Above them, an eagle soared on the airwaves, a high-pitched, prolonged cry resounding through the air as it came to rest on a giant pine bordering the eastern edge of the pasture. Tucked into a branch next to the trunk lay a large nest, interwoven with sticks, grasses, and moss. In it sat his mate and their two eaglets. Unclear about much in their new world, which expanded by the day, the llamas settled into innocence, trusting if they needed to know anything, a sign would come with the sound of an engine, or thirst that would remind them to go to the creek for water. The eagle's call stirred a deep sense of remembering within them, a knowing that as life moved forward, the sacred revealed itself, relentless in its unfolding. In the meantime, Domingo and Bacardi sat on the hillside like royalty, watching over their new world.

Jimmy scowled as they pulled up to the front of the small church, complete with a steeple.

"Look at this, Jimmy. It's so cool." Katherine hugged him. "It'll be okay, eh?"

"Well, I hope we're not delivering babies on the church pew." He opened the car door and helped her out.

"Oh look, there's Martha." Liza got out and waved her over. "So glad you're here. Jimmy's a little nervous."

"I'll keep an eye on them." Martha went over and said hello. "Any contractions yet?"

"No," Katherine said. "I have more energy today than I've had in a while. It feels wonderful to be out and about."

"Hmmm…" Martha mused. "Right before birth, it's common for a woman to have a burst of energy. Sit close to me. You can squeeze my hand if anything changes."

"Hey, it's the happy wanderer." Old Max came up and slapped Jimmy on the back, then shook Henry's hand. "This is great! Now, if that minister would let me play my harmonica with the choir." He pulled it out of his pocket and played a short trill.

"You've been practicing." Jimmy chuckled at Helen's frown a few feet away. "Gotta work on sounding a little more angelic though." Max followed Jimmy's glance.

"Good morning, Helen." Max smoothed his hair back and made a little bow.

Helen started to smile, then pulled her lips tight and walked away.

"Still as charming as ever." Jimmy fake-punched Max in the arm.

"Been trying to talk to that woman for years." Max shrugged his shoulders. "Maybe she just needs to be serenaded." He patted the harmonica in his pocket and grinned.

Settled in the pews, halfway through the sermon, Liza nudged Henry at the sound of a soft snore. He jerked awake in his seat just as the minister made the final announcements, welcoming Jimmy home and Katherine to the community. Jimmy stood and offered Katherine a hand up, who blushed as everyone in the church clapped and those nearby reached out to shake her and Jimmy's hand.

A bit later at the potluck, Henry and Jimmy talked with the farmers who had llamas for predator control. "Easy to care for, keeps the coyotes away."

At that moment, Jimmy looked at Katherine, plate in hand as Liza introduced her to Helen. Katherine's eyes got big as she put her plate on the table and grabbed Liza's arm. He looked down to see a puddle of water between her feet.

"Pop, get the car." Jimmy reached Katherine at the same time as Martha.

"I think it's starting," Katherine grimaced as her belly contracted. Martha put her hand on Katherine and timed the contraction.

"First one?" Martha asked, looking down as Helen put a towel over the puddle. "And it looks like your water broke as well."

"Yes, to both." Katherine sighed as the contraction relaxed.

"Pop's getting the car," Jimmy stammered. "Can we make it home, or should we go to the hospital?"

"No, Jimmy, not the hospital." Katherine begged.

"We should be able to make it home," Martha said. "Her contractions just started. Jimmy, can you drive my car, and we'll go with Henry?"

"Sure, anything…" He took the keys from her.

"I made a mess on the floor," Katherine said. "I need…"

"Don't you worry," Helen said. "I'll take care of it."

With a smile of gratitude, Katherine let Liza and Martha guide her to the car. Seconds after Katherine settled into the back seat, another contraction hit.

"So, that's eleven minutes since the first one." Martha put her arm around Katherine. "Breathe with it dear. We'll be fine." She looked over as Jimmy passed them on the two-lane country road. "Easy, boy. That's my car."

"He drives fast when he's excited," Liza said from the front.

"Sorry," Katherine mumbled. Martha squeezed her hand, then made the sign of a cross over her heart.

Five thousand miles to the south, high in the mountains of Peru, a butterfly perched on King Llama's nose. He flicked his ears and wrinkled his nose, but the glistening purples and blues of its silky wings, metamorphosed from the chrysalis that once cradled it, caught the sun and scattered light like sparks of magic, carefree in its newfound freedom of flight.

King Llama heard Little Sister Mountain Putucusi's giggle at the playfulness of this new spirit. The butterfly lifted from his nose and drifted into the breeze, reveling in the joy of gliding over terraces and peaks, a luminous thread woven into the tapestry of all things. And in that moment, the world exhaled, as it had done for centuries, in quiet reverence for the dance of all things.

SEVENTEEN

Jimmy waited with the kitchen door open as Henry pulled up. "Whoa, that was a close one." He wiped the sweat off his brow, then helped Katherine out of the back seat.

"Who's having this baby, anyway, son?" Henry asked.

Jimmy's cheeks turned red. "Sorry. I've never done this before."

As they entered the house, Katherine came to a sudden stop, gasping as she clutched her belly. Jimmy paled, eyes big. "What should I do?"

"Just breathe," Martha said, coming in with her medical bag, looking at the second hand on her watch. "Forty-five seconds. Let's help this young lady up to bed." She handed Liza a piece of paper with a phone number on it. "Can you give Dr. Joe a call? Let him know we need him?"

"Of course." Liza, hat still on her head and leather bag hanging off her arm, picked up the phone and, with nervous fingers, dialed the numbers. "Then I'll be up. Henry, put coffee on, will ya?"

"Sure, Liza." Henry jumped on the task, relieved to have a purpose amidst the chaos.

Minutes later, Liza and Henry came up the stairs and into the bedroom. Jimmy stood frozen at the side of the bed, helpless as Katherine grimaced, tears and sweat rolling down her face as another contraction gripped her. "My back. Hurts so bad."

"Jimmy," Martha said.

"Yes. Anything. What?"

"Climb up on the bed behind Katherine, like I explained earlier." She grinned at Liza as Jimmy wiggled himself on the bed, careful of Katherine like she was a fragile China bowl. "Now, scoot up with your back to the wall, and let Katherine lean into you. With the next contraction, rub her back and hips, and breathe with her, like you practiced. Remember?"

"Yeah, got it." Eyes wide, flushed and perspiring, he held his breath, waiting for the next contraction.

"Breathe, Jimmy," Katherine said. "You're making me nervous."

Liza and Henry chuckled in the background. "Need anything, Martha?"

Martha looked around the room, satisfied that everything she needed was in arm's reach, her medical bag on the table next to her. "How about a basin of warm water?"

"Right away," Lisa said, heading into the bathroom, basin in hand.

"Here," Henry said. "Let me carry it over." Liza grinned and nodded.

"Here we go, Jimmy," Martha said, as Katherine's belly tightened with another contraction. "Rub her back and breathe with her.

"In through our nose, one, two, three, four." Jimmy demonstrated with his breath as he coached her. "Hold it … now purse your lips and blow out. We got this, hon."

Martha grinned. "Good job."

"How do you stay so relaxed?" he asked Martha, holding his arms around Katherine as she closed her eyes, relaxing into him between contractions.

"It's the most natural thing in the world. I've seen a birth or two. Ok, here comes another."

"One, two, three, four… good job, honey. Blow out through your lips."

"If you need to push, Katherine, go ahead and bear down. Your contractions are about 4 minutes apart, so we're moving right along." Martha looked up as Dr. Joe came into the room.

"Hey, everyone! Ready to have some babies?" The doctor buttoned up his white coat and grinned at the sight before him. "How's everything coming along, Martha?"

"Contractions are closer. Oh, here comes another. Doing great, Jimmy. That one was three minutes. These babies are in a hurry!"

Dr. Joe chuckled as Martha got up and he eased into the chair. "Gloves?"

"Right here, dear." Dr. Joe hummed as he examined Katherine, then looked up, meeting the intense stare of Katherine and Jimmy. "I see a crown. Won't be long now."

Martha sat on the side of the bed to monitor contractions. "Never gets old, does it, Dr. Joe?"

"Never."

Liza walked over to the bed and offered Jimmy a glass of water. "Oh, thanks. Geez, I'm so thirsty." Chugging it, he held it out to his mom. "Katherine, are you thirsty?" He looked over at Martha. "Is it okay?"

"Yes, small sips of water are fine." Jimmy took the refilled glass from his mom and helped Katherine to drink.

"Oh, man, that's the best." She smiled as Liza wiped the sweat off her forehead with a cloth. "Thank you, it was getting in my eyes. Oh," she took in a deep breath. "Here we go." This time, her breath came faster as fresh perspiration beaded on her forehead.

"We got this, Katherine." Jimmy fell in stride with her breathing, almost panting now.

"I see a head." Dr. Joe said. "Next contraction, Katherine, bear down and push." Her face a mixture of pain and excitement, Katherine groaned in relief as Jimmy rubbed her back and hips. "So good," she whispered.

"More water, hon?"

"No, let's finish this."

"Here we go." Martha held her hand on Katherine's belly. "Okay guys, deep breath in as the contraction builds…. deeper, deeper. Now bear down, Katherine, and push."

Katherine cried out, taking another breath in, then squinched her face up and pushed with all her might."

"We got this," Jimmy cried with her. "Another breath, there ya go."

Katherine pushed one last time, then collapsed in Jimmy's arms.

"Here's number one." Dr. Joe placed the baby in the soft blanket that Martha held out. "You have a little girl, kids."

"Ten fingers, ten toes." Martha wrapped the baby, whose whimper turned into a wail, taking in the first few breaths outside of her mother's womb. "Liza, can you hold her so we can baby welcome baby number two?"

"Oh, my, yes!"

"Let us see, Mom," Jimmy said. Liza held the baby so Jimmy and Katherine could see. "So beautiful. Have you thought of a name yet?"

"Christina," Katherine said.

"Oh…" Liza's eyes filled with tears.

"Ready for number two?" Dr. Joe asked.

As the last contraction hit, Katherine used her breath to relax and push, feeling Jimmy in time with her.

"Push Katherine, push." Dr. Joe called out.

"Arghhh…" Katherine cried, sweat and tears pouring down her face, hair damp, sticking to her skin.

"Faster, Katherine." Jimmy exaggerated panting breaths. "Good job, hon." Katherine cried out with the last push.

"Ah," Dr. Joe said, cradling the newborn in his arms. "Christina has a brother. Martha, got a blanket?"

"Yes." She held it out. "Ten fingers, ten toes. Here's your babies." Liza and Martha sat on either side of the couple, cradling the babies in their arms. Jimmy wiggled out from behind Katherine, then lay beside her with the babies between them. Together they unwrapped them, counted their fingers and toes again, then grinned at each other.

"And the little fellow, what will his name be?" Martha asked.

"Jimmy, Jr..," Katherine and Jimmy said at the same time.

"Beautiful. Okay, Katherine, ready to finish up?" Dr. Joe asked. "One more big push. There ya go, perfect. Joe tied off the umbilical cord. "You didn't tear, so no stitches were needed. Great job, Katherine."

"Thank you." Katherine put her head on the pillow and closed her eyes. "I might need to take a nap."

Martha and Liza took the babies to the changing table and, with warm rags from the basin, washed them. Henry came over and peered down over Liza's shoulder. "Seems like yesterday." Liza smiled at him.

Martha brought the scale over. "Let's weigh them. Christina first."

Liza put the baby on the scale.

"Five pounds, seven ounces." She wrapped her up in the blanket, then weighed Jimmy Jr. "Five pounds, five ounces. You have a little football player, Jimmy." Martha went over to Katherine. "Ready to feed them? Get your milk flowing?"

"Yes, and then I'll sleep."

"I think we all need a nap," Henry said.

"Good, strong, healthy babies," Dr. Joe announced. "Martha, I'll leave the birth certificates here on the table. Have Katherine and Jimmy sign them, and we'll register them with the county clerk in the morning."

"Righto," Martha said. "You off?"

"Yes, I'm going to the hospital to make rounds. Might have another birth tonight."

"Busy day."

"Babies have their own schedule." He chuckled. "Congratulations. You did a great job and have beautiful little ones. May God bless all of you with a long and healthy life."

"Thank you, Dr. Joe."

Martha nestled Christina up to Katherine's breast, who clamped on hungrily. "Well, she didn't need any instructions. A little at a time, or you'll get sore." Katherine nodded as Martha put Jimmy Jr. to her other breast. He scrunched his tiny nose around, pursing his lips, but once Martha guided his mouth over Katherine's nipple, he clamped on.

"How often do they need to nurse?"

"They'll set their own schedule, but every couple of hours. Eating and sleeping will consume most of their days. And yours." Martha picked up the basin.

"Here, let me." Henry took the basin to the bathroom while Liza cleaned up. Martha examined Katherine. "You're all set. Pads are in the bathroom. If you have pain that gets worse or any questions, Liza has our number. Call anytime. Otherwise, I'll be out to see you first thing in the morning."

"Thanks, Martha. Wow is all I can say."

After the twins finished nursing, Liza wrapped up the babies and nestled them into the cradle. She and Henry stood for the longest time, looking at them and then at the bed to the sleeping couple. They tiptoed out of the room.

"I'll start dinner. They'll be hungry when they wake up." She looked up at Henry, who seemed at a loss for words. "Everything okay, dear?"

"I love you, Liza." He said.

"We have grandbabies, Henry. Christina and Jimmy Jr."

The early morning sun shone bright, the air crisp as Domingo and Bacardi wandered through the pasture. It had been a while since they heard the sound of an engine. They liked the grass well enough, but apples and carrots pleased them more.

As they explored the seemingly endless horizon, the llamas stopped and held their nose to the air as if the breeze might whisper news of things to come. They couldn't name what that meant in their short lives, but the wind spoke in a language they trusted.

Following the tree line, they found a narrow trail that led through a patch of woods and into another broad pasture. A familiar scent stirred their senses, and with delight, their noses guided them to a grove of apple and pear trees.

Bacardi nosed a pear off the ground, but halted mid-chomp, juice glistening on his nose, looking over at a rustle in the grass. Mother Fox peeked from behind an apple tree, several feet away, wary that these new beings were encroaching on even more of her realm.

Their eyes met and held. In that stillness, something ancient stirred, an unspoken pact. The land embraced all. The tall grass, the fast-running stream, even the two-legged's who offered sweet gifts. They would respect each other.

As understanding deepened, reflected in the softening of their eyes, the grass beside Mother Fox quivered, dotted with the curious eyes and noses of her kits.

Bacardi chuckled with a flicker of his ears, bringing a smile to King Llama and Little Sister Mountain Putucusi, five thousand miles to the south.

The message carried on the wind, clear and timeless:

All will be well.

EIGHTEEN

Late afternoon, Claud pulled off Highway 99 and into a service station. She sat in her car, staring at the pay phone, torn between being a dutiful daughter and her reluctance to get dragged into the familiar guilt trip that came with it.

Bakersfield and her mother were an hour away. Tired after grinding through LA traffic, she sighed and rummaged through the glove box, digging out change. Unable to reach her mother in earlier attempts, as each quarter dropped with a clink into the metal box, part of her wished there would be no answer, but on the fifth ring, Claud heard the familiar voice.

"Hi, Mom."

"Claudette. Are you coming home?"

"I'm thinking about a visit, Mom."

"I would love that. There's a young man at church you could meet, a solid Christian boy. He'd take care of you. And the local hospital is lovely, you'd land a job there in a second."

Claud's stomach sank. All the reasons she left home and joined the Army flooded through her brain. She stuttered. "I'm. I'm mm … I only wanted to say hello. Maybe…."

"Oh, please come, Claudette, that is your name after all. No more of this Claud business. Come home. You can settle down here and stop living such a reckless life."

"I know, Mom. I know." Claud took a breath. "I appreciate that." Silence hung in the air.

Through the sweetness in her mother's voice, judgement crept in.

Reckless… she doesn't have a clue about my life since I left… and what's wrong with Claud?

Across the road a sign lit up: Topper Motor Hotel – Rooms $7.99. "Mom, I promise. I'm just getting settled back into a routine here. I'll come soon. I love you, Mom."

Claud hung up the phone, her mother's raised voice echoing through the air: "Now you listen to me young lady…" She pressed the receiver down on the cradle, disconnecting, her heart too raw right now to deal with her mother. She would go to Oregon and maybe come back for a visit. Her mother's voice lived in her head, always judging, always critical, but over the past couple of years, she began to see another way. Headed for the hotel, waiting for the light to change, Claud rested her hand on Chris's pack which rode in the front seat like a fellow traveler.

How I wish it was you and I… going to Oregon for a new life together like we planned. Even my mother would have loved you.

A whispering breeze wove through the trees on Little Sister Mountain Putucusi, a dance of luminous threads, woven together in fleeting brilliance, only to dissolve and reform anew, each moment a testament to the inherent beauty of the universe.

King llama stood above the city at the Sun Gate, beholding miracles that continued to fall into place. Once a shadow in the cave, Chris expanded into the colors of the rainbow and back again into the familiar earthbound form, infinite light rippling out, touching hearts. He appeared as if by magic beside King Llama, casting a light woven with yellow, green, and purple hues around them.

Body aching from sitting cramped in the small car all day, Claud soaked in the hot bath. Relaxed and settled into an overly soft mattress, it felt like she was nestled in soft clouds floating slowly through the universe. Time in Vietnam, the horror of war mingled with the miracle of skills that on occasion revived life, or a smile before death, wove through her restless sleep. Chris drifted into her dream. He wore a rainbow cloak, swirling it around her, much like a magician would. Reaching out to touch him, her hands moved through a light which warmed her heart, a heart that had been tentative and cold since the day she stood and saluted his casket as it rolled by, absent of emotion in the efficacy of the military. Awake long before the sun, and ready to follow the dream, Claud continued her journey north.

NINETEEN

Dewdrops from a crisp, new dawn sparkled like diamonds on Domingo and Bacardi's thick, wool coat. Barely one hundred pounds, each day brought new understanding of being in a physical body as their legs grew stronger and bodies larger. Curiosity and innocence, a driving force inherited from ancestors, moved them into each day with an openness to the unknown of many possibilities. On this new morning, the strength of their lineage flowed through their bloodstream like a river, bringing with it a readiness, and a quiet knowing of their deepening world. Sitting along the tree line, their bellies hugged the earth, connected with all things, holding steady as new vibrations informed them of changes coming.

Katherine stretched into the sunlight streaming through the window, savoring the warmth as it flowed through her limbs. The babies nursed at four, so perhaps she might have a moment to enjoy a trip to the bathroom without interruption.

"Coffee and toast to start your day?" Liza entered, setting a tray on the bedside stand. "It's a beautiful morning."

"I love the view." She picked up the cup, the steam rising off the top tickling her nose. "I love the early morning sun. Have you seen Jimmy?"

"He and Henry went to check on the llamas. They're thinking of building a shelter out there for them." Liza peeked into the bassinets. "Little miracles."

"Mmmm, so good, eh?" Katherine sipped her coffee. "We're getting into a routine. They're nursing every three or four hours. Hoping Jimmy can help me with a bath, but I'm sure I can manage."

"I'll start the water." Liza disappeared into the bathroom, appearing a moment later. "These old clawfoot tubs are wonderful for a soak, but you almost need a ladder to climb in." She peeked out the curtains. "Here they are now."

Footsteps on the creaky stairs announced Jimmy, who poked his head in the door.

"Shoosh… I want them to sleep a little longer. Help me with the bath, eh?"

Liza stood at the door, her heart full of love for her son and his new family. Across the hall, the boy's old bedroom transformed into a nursery. Her eyes drifted to the corner, to the spot where Chris's bed once stood, unchanged since they were toddlers, until now. Loss seeped into the cracks of the new joy, creating a mosaic, much like the rivers of veins and arteries that ran throughout her body, creating a place where a heart could heal.

"I can't wait to introduce the babies to the llamas," Katherine said, nestling into the hot water. "First coffee, now this."

"Bacardi and Domingo are such curious beings," Jimmy mused. "Llamas, babies…" He gazed at the new lives he and Katherine created, little innocent beings in the bassinettes, a mirror of him and Chris, now responsible in their new world to keep the lineage strong.

Katherine came out of the bathroom, tying the blue, checkered flannel robe, her hair tousled in a bun on top of her head.

120

He stood speechless, staring at her beauty. Their eyes met in a timeless moment of heart-filled desire where no secrets lay. "Are you happy?" she asked.

Jimmy closed his eyes and took a deep breath. "I'm happy, I am … things are just moving so fast." His eyes gentled as cooing sounds arose from the bassinet. "And Christina is awake." He reached down, meeting her tiny fingers in the air. "Are you ready for her?"

Katherine settled on the bed and opened the robe, baring her breast and holding out her arms. As suckling sounds filled the air, Jimmy Jr. woke with gurgles on the precipice of a cry. "Just like his papa, doesn't want to miss any of the action."

Jimmy went to the bassinet, wrinkling his nose. "Whew! That's a strong one." He made faces at his son while changing his diaper, then snugged him in a blanket. With Jimmy Jr. cradled in his arms, he plopped down on the bed beside Katherine. "Ready for number two?"

"Yes." Katherine ran her fingers through her babies downy hair as Jimmy Jr. nestled at her free breast. "It felt good to sleep a few hours between feedings."

A knock on the door brought Dr Joe and Martha, grinning at the sight of the happy family camped out on the bed. Tummies full, Jimmy took the sleepy twins and one by one nestled them into the bassinets while Dr Joe examined Katherine.

"Doing okay?" The Doctor peered over his glasses, gentle blue eyes inquisitive.

"Feeding these two every couple hours and sleeping in between. No pain, bleeding is slowing up. I had a bath." She smiled. "Renewed for another day."

Martha tugged two colorful strips of cloth out of her bag. "I brought you slings to carry the babies. It'll make it easier to navigate those stairs when you're ready to get out and about."

"We used these in Canada." Katherine unfolded the triangle cloths, running her fingers over colorful designs of rainbows and unicorns. "I can't wait to take Christina and Jimmy Jr. to meet the llamas."

"Join us for breakfast?" Liza popped her head in. "Freddy called and he's tied up in surgery all day but will be out tonight. Got plenty."

"Thanks anyway," Martha said. "We're booked solid."

"Hand me a baby." Katherine draped a cloth around her, knotting it on her shoulder. A few moments later, with one baby snug in the sling, she turned to Jimmy. "That works. Now, your turn."

The aroma of bacon, scrambled eggs and a fresh pot of coffee greeted the new family as they followed Dr Joe and Martha down the stairs. "Oh, look at you." Liza beamed. "That was kind of you, Martha."

"My pleasure." Martha winked at Katherine. "I know you're itching to visit those llamas. We'll be back in the morning to see how you're doing." And with a wave and a smile, the doctor and his wife went about their day.

Liza jumped at the shrill ring of the phone. "Get that, Henry? My hands are full."

"This is amazing." Katherine nuzzled the downy crown of her son. "We're hungry."

"Can you talk to Helen?" Henry called out, stretching the long cord over to Liza, who cradled it against her ear, holding it with her shoulder.

"Yes, Helen, we have twins. Christina and Jimmy, Jr." Softness filled her face as she listened. "That would be lovely.

Tomorrow morning?" She winked at Henry, who held up the counter, eavesdropping. "I'll have the coffee on. I'll tell them." She shook the phone off her shoulder, Henry catching it as the eggs neatly slid out of the pan and onto the platter.

Claud squirmed in the driver's seat and glanced at her watch. Only noon, but she'd been on the road eight hours, much longer than she was used to sitting anywhere. Dreading the thought of another five hours in the car, she fiddled with the radio dial.

"Welcome to the Casey Kasem top forty." The road blurred before her, memories pulling her back to that day in Vietnam.

Air hot and oppressive, she'd held down a table in a dark corner of the air base bar, sipping an ice-cold beer. Alcohol was a forbidden luxury for the sparse medical staff, who could be called back in at a moment's notice. It had been a tough day in the medic tent. A soldier she couldn't save, using his last breaths to tell her about his young wife and baby at home, floating out of this life with a smile on his face as he whispered their names. She lifted the glass and forgot for a second as the cold liquid trickled down her throat. Behind the bar a transistor radio asked her to stay tuned for Casey's top forty.

"Coming in at twenty-five of the top forty is Bette Midler – Do Ya Want to Dance..."

She sensed him before looking up. Chris stood there with his hand out, taking in her day, understanding. Gliding across the floor, held in his arms, she felt safe, something she hadn't experienced much in her life. No words were necessary.

The blast of a horn passing jerked her back into reality. A giant green and white sign flashed by, welcoming her to Oregon. This morning when she got into the car, Claud thought for certain her destiny lay before her. Now, with her hand resting on his pack, that late afternoon in Vietnam was the only destiny she wanted.

Winding up the incline of Interstate Five, Claud slowed at the following sign: Siskiyou Mountain Summit, elevation four thousand, three hundred and ten feet. She swerved into the exit lane without thinking, ignoring the blast of another horn, and pulled into a shady spot near the lookout point.

"Just you and me, kid." She pulled the green Army bag out of the front seat and lugged it to a nearby rock with a panoramic view. Rereading the letters, her fingers traced the ink on the paper, feeling his touch. Claud wasn't sure she could give them up, but she needed to. Any parent of someone as special as Chris deserved closure.

Stomach growling, she stopped at the local tourist trap. A bottle of Orange Crush and a bag of peanuts in hand, Claud got back on the road. If she kept the pedal to the metal, she could make McMinnville before dark, drop off the pack and finally allow destiny to inform her of the next step.

The Star Seeds, once bouncing balls of energy, crossing mountains, oceans and prairies only days ago, were now young llama beings in Henry and Liza's pasture. They walked the creek, slurping in icy cold water which soothed their throats. Always alert for the sound of a motor, tractor or truck, sure to bring the sweetness of apples and carrots, they navigated their new territory. Babes in a brand-new world, their curiosity drove them forward with each sunrise, to the promise and possibility of each new day.

Mother Fox and her babies, the rightful claimants of this land before Domingo and Bacardi arrived, moved through the grass, a bit wary yet curious all the same. Much like the Starseeds, the kits grew since the day Domingo surprised himself, and them, by spitting green, foul-smelling bile all over one of the kits. Life was unfolding in unexpected ways for all those inhabiting the earth, creating ripples of change throughout the world, unbeknownst to the average person going through their day.

Claud wove through rush hour traffic as she neared Portland. Eyes blurry from hours on the road, she rested her hand on the green Army pack in the passenger seat, unable to imagine it not being there riding shotgun. Six months ago, the war ended, and she stepped back onto American soil. Numb, raw and nurturing a broken heart, she hadn't given a lot of thought to Chris's parents who surely would be grateful to have the letters from their son. They would have received the infamous knock on the door, and upon opening, the faces of the Army Officer and Army Chaplin. Duty-bound, compassionate yet neutral, the faces on the other side of the knock said it all.

Next exit McMinnville, the one she needed to take. Would they hate her? Claud knew she'd waited too long to give the letters back. A good girl, she followed the rules. A cold sweat covered her face as she turned on the blinker and followed the road.

Cruising down Main Street, she pulled into the Standard gas station, which appeared to be the only one in town. A scruffy grey-haired man secured the pumps for the night. He gave her a friendly wave but the look on his face said he was ready to close and looking forward to a cold one before heading home. She pulled over and rolled down her window.

"I'm sorry to bother you, but could you give directions?" Claud pulled a letter out and held it up. Max squinted at the envelope, eyes widening at Chris's name in the return address. He looked at the woman in the car, ready to burst into tears at any minute.

"I'm Max." Wiping greasy hands on his overalls, his face broadened into a smile. "Henry and Liza Muller are old friends."

Relief flooded her face.

"You family?"

"Family?" Claud stammered. "No … I knew their son in Vietnam. I brought his things. They don't know I'm coming." Her eyes filled with panic. "I only made the decision to come yesterday."

Max saw lots of things come and go in this town and the loss of one of their own to Vietnam rocked their little community. Fingers crossed that her intentions were honorable, he gave her directions. "Easy to find. Need gas or a cold drink before you head over?"

"No thanks. I've been on the road since early this morning." Her voice trembled. "I want to get this over with. I'm sure dredging up memories will be hard on them."

"They're good people," Max said. "Hold on a minute, would ya?"

"Sure." Her stomach fluttered with nervousness as he hurried into the gas station and picked up a phone. *Great, he's calling to warn them, or the police.* Heart racing, she waited. A few minutes later, he came out and handed her a piece of paper. "This here is Bonnie's Boarding House. I called and she has a room, so I told her to hang onto it for you." He smiled. "It'll be okay. She said to get there as late as you need, it's a good TV night, so she'll be up."

"I don't know what to say."

"We take care of our own around here. I knew Chris and Jimmy from their first day on earth. Quite the gift you're bringing. They'll appreciate it. Come back in the morning and I'll fill up your car. On the house."

"Thank you." She looked in the rear-view mirror as she waited to turn out onto the street, wondering if everyone in this town was nice like Max.

126

TWENTY

Mist drifted over the Lost City of Light, shrouding its stone sanctuaries as the sun began its descent into the west, making way for the moon. King Llama marveled at the day, each one uniquely different.

Today brought many souls in search of healing. Some arrived with broken hearts, while others carried a quiet ache of regret, believing they'd failed life. The mountains welcomed them all, holding their sorrows within the folds of ancient terraces, allowing time and earth to weave a new purpose. It was the children who delighted King Llama the most. Unburdened by the weight of years, they moved through the world with innocence, their souls open and attuned to the unseen. Eyes wide and open to wonder, they wandered the sacred city, their laughter drifting through the morning air like wind chimes in a soft breeze.

Jimmy parted the yellow gingham curtains of the kitchen window and gazed at the land he grew up on. Little Christina snugged into the sling against his chest, he could almost feel his twin brother standing next to him, celebrating the moment. Born of the same womb twenty-eight years ago, like branching stems from a single flower, he and Chris had always felt both inseparable and distinct, each a part of the other, yet wholly his own.

"Hey, Jimmy," Henry called. "You're up." From his earliest memories, playing Canasta was one of the best. A lovely family most of the time, the teeth came out at the sound of shuffling cards. Grinning at the memory, he turned to the lively voices in the living room, but in the distance, saw a light flash in the sun from the mirror of a car coming down the gravel driveway. Freddy arrived before dinner, they weren't expecting anyone, and dusk was near.

"Car coming?" Henry called.

"Someone's probably lost. I'll handle it, Pop."

A gold Pinto pulled up, and a young woman, blond hair casually tossed on top of her head in a red plastic clip, stepped out. She reached into the car, pulling out a large green bag. Comforted by the touch of Katherine's hand on his shoulder, he answered the door on the first knock.

Paralyzed, Claud stared at Jimmy. The same face, same eyes. Her entire life shifted when she met Chris, ending when she saluted the casket carrying his body, one of so many lost during a senseless war. And now, he stood in front of her. Unsure she could handle one more life upheaval, she froze, staring. Claud saw lips moving, but didn't hear. Dropping the duffle bag in the doorway, she turned and ran back to her car.

"Wait," Jimmy called. He saw the words Army and Christopher Muller stamped on the bag. "Wait, please!" Claud stopped mid-step, fingers on the door handle of her car.

Katherine stepped over and, without words, yet with perfect understanding, put her arm around Claud. "I'm new to the family as well. Heck, I haven't even been here for two weeks. It'll be okay."

"I… I… I wanted to bring letters I found in a box. I… I… thought his parents would want them." Claud looked up to the sound of Jimmy's footsteps.

"Chris and I used to get that all the time. Being an identical twin can be tricky, or fun." He winked at her, relieved when a flicker of recognition softened the panic in her eyes. "You met my brother in Vietnam?"

"Yes," Claud stammered, her voice catching. "I knew he had a twin. I just didn't know you would..." Eyes filling, she whispered. "We were going to marry as soon as the war ended. He's supposed to be standing here with me now... instead I only have..." She gestured to the green army bag laying on the door stoop.

"Won't you come in and tell us about it?" Katherine asked, rocking baby Jimmy Jr. in the sling. The soft baby sounds eased the tension.

Claud took a tentative step towards the house as Henry came into the kitchen, stopping dead in his tracks at the sight of the green duffle bag sitting in the doorway, his eyes locking on the black stamped words: ARMY - CHRISTOPHER MULLER.

"What is it?" Liza froze at her husband's gaze. "Henry?"

"I don't know." They went past the door and stopped at the sight of Jimmy and Katherine with their arms around a terrified young woman.

"We have a guest," Katherine said, guiding the young woman into the house.

"This is Claud. She drove from San Diego to bring you this." Jimmy picked up the duffle bag and brought it in, plunking it down on the dining room table.

"You must be tired young lady. That's a long drive." Henry took in the terror on Claud's face, not knowing a thing, yet knowing everything.

Liza took Claud's hands. "Come in and sit down. We made a fresh pot of tea, and there's plenty of dinner left on the stove."

Freddy stood to go, hesitant to impose on the moment. Growing up, life in flux was common in the big San Francisco house. His parents loved having their home abuzz with musicians, hippies and political activists coming and going, but he'd never seen so many new beginnings in one place in such a short time. Unsure if he should stay, curiosity made him sit back down.

Claud looked around at the friendly faces, eyes stopping briefly on Freddy's face, feeling the room's warmth. Her stomach grumbled at the smells coming from the kitchen. Relaxing slightly, she asked: "Could I use your bathroom?"

Fog drifted through the ancient stone city, weaving like a living spirit between terraces and temples, softening jagged peaks as streams of gold and violet streaked through the sky. Late afternoon shadows stretched across the city and mist curled around the stone houses, softening their edges as if blurring the lines between worlds. In the fading light, a rainbow curved across the deep gorge and back again, and in a shimmer of iridescence, it shifted—morphing into human form.

"Did you like that?" Chris's voice moved through the air like a shimmer, not carried by sound but borne on the currents of thought, as if whispered by the wind.

King Llama's ears flicked in amusement. "Your colors are beautiful," he said. "Perhaps one day, those you love will look to the sky, and the rainbow will remind them of you and all who have crossed over to the mountain tops."

Chris's form glowed for a moment, pulsing with knowing. "It's happening, isn't it?"

"Yes, son," King Llama said, his voice as steady as the mountains.

TWENTY-ONE

Liza turned to the click of the lock on the bathroom door. "You must be starving. Would you like dinner? Or a cup of tea? I have a fresh pot of Bigelow Constant Comment. Won't keep us awake."

"Just tea, please," Claud said. "I can't stay long."

"Ok, dear." Liza smiled gently. "Go, have a seat with the others. I'll bring it in."

Rapt eyes turned to Claud when she entered the living room. Unsure what to expect, kindness wasn't high on the list. Her hair came loose, and she fiddled with it, wrapping it around her finger, wondering where to start.

"Tell us about Chris." Liza put the tea pot on the coffee table and poured Claud a cup. "I brought a plate of sandwiches and cookies if you decide you're hungry."

Claud reached for a sandwich, the simple act steadying her nerves. "I'm a nurse. I joined the Army and in an impulsive moment, signed up for a tour of duty in Vietnam. I'd been there for about eight months with a few weeks left when I met Chris. Rumors were flying that the war would end soon." Settled in, her eyes sparkled at the retelling of seeing him in the medic tent after his jeep got hit by lightning. "It was love at first sight and we dated military style, fast and furious. Thinking the war would end soon, we planned to marry once we were stateside. Claud paused, biting her lip, her voice a whisper. "But of course that never happened.

The night before Chris died, we danced at the little bar on base where they played music on a transistor radio. Next morning, Chris and his buddies were lacing their boots when a renegade mortar shell hit their barracks. Tears streamed down her face, mirroring Henry and Liza's. "None of them made it out alive. Later that week we were told to pack up. We were coming home."

Hands trembling, the cup teetered as she set it in the saucer, drops of tea sloshing over the side. Claud went over to the table and opened Chris's duffle, her fingers pausing on Chris's name, stamped on the green canvas. "His captain knew we planned to be married and asked if I wanted his bag. Last week I started going through things and found these." She pulled out the letters and handed them to Liza. "I'm sorry I didn't bring them to you sooner. I'm not sure what else is there but you should have it."

Henry and Liza stared at the letters, the familiar handwriting on the front of the envelope and looked up at Claud, eyes wet. "This means everything to us, young lady," Henry said.

Liza reached into the bag, pulling out a tee shirt, running her fingers over the soft cotton, then held it to her heart as she leaned into Henry's welcoming arm. "It's his smell… like you brought him back to us."

"Care if we have a look at these letters?" Henry asked.

"Of course. They're yours." She took in the emotion-filled faces. "I can't stay long…"

"I have an idea," Freddy said. "Do you like llamas?"

Claud's brow furrowed. "Llamas? Certainly didn't expect that question in a million years."

Jimmy laughed. "Freddy is our local veterinarian. He's looking after some llamas that showed up the other day."

"Out of thin air!" Henry said. "Like magic."

"And it's been nothing but blessings ever since." Liza beamed through glistening eyes. "Meeting Freddy… Jimmy came home, we have new grandbabies, and now we have you. All since the llamas came."

"Perhaps the llamas brought the joy and blessings," Katherine said softly. "It's… I don't know how to describe it." She shrugged. "Henry's right… magic."

"Now all we need is a dog," Jimmy said. "And we have hungry babies, it seems." He jostled little Christina in the sling.

"It'll be dark soon," Freddy said. "Want to come along and check on the llamas with me? They can read the letters and let it all soak in. Won't take long."

Katherine took in the exchange between Freddy and Claud, her gaze lingering for a moment before she turned to Liza with a knowing smile.

Claud stammered. Nothing she rehearsed had meaning here. "I've got a room in town at…" She dug in her pocket for the paper Max gave her.

"Let me guess," Freddy said. "Bonnie's Boarding House?"

"Yes, how did you know?" She unfolded the paper, handing it to him.

"Only place in town," Freddy laughed. "Ride out with me and check the llamas…"

"Domingo and Bacardi, you mean." Liza nudged Freddy with her elbow.

"Yes," Freddy grinned. "After you meet Domingo and Bacardi, we'll swing back here, and you can follow me into town. I'll get you to Bonnie's."

"Well, okay then." Claud stood. "The last thing I expected today was to meet llamas, but I guess that's what's happening."

"Why don't you come out for breakfast tomorrow? We'd love to get to know you better," Liza said.

"You have no idea what this means." Jimmy put his hand on Claud's shoulder, tipping her chin up. "Losing Chris, well, I only found out a few days ago, and it still hasn't quite set in."

"I'm glad I came," Claud whispered. Katherine hugged her as gurgling turned to whimpers from Jimmy Jr.

"Looks like we have babies to deal with." Katherine pinched her nose. "Whoa. Diaper time as well. Please come tomorrow."

"I'd love to," Claud said.

On an upper terrace of the sacred city, King Llama bent his knees to the earth. The soft grass cradled him as he eased his hindquarters down, sinking into the embrace of the land.

"It is a beautiful thing," murmured Little Sister Mountain Putucusi, her voice woven into the evening breeze which always arrived right before the stars. Chris stood in the folds of her trees, shifting in and out of human form, absorbed in the life which was marching forward in the house he grew up in, shimmering in love for everyone there.

"All will be well," King Llama whispered, his voice low and certain, a vow as old as the mountains themselves. The first stars pierced the velvet sky, and the world exhaled, cradled in the knowing that all things, seen and unseen, past and present, were held in the embrace of time, love, and the ever-turning dance of the earth.

Lisa and Henry sat hand in hand on the couch, the letters open on the table, having been read multiple times.

"Babies asleep?" Liza asked.

"Yeah," Jimmy picked up the letter addressed to him and plopped down in the rose-colored easy chair. "Fed, diapered, and sound asleep, as is my wife."

"Freddy and Claud swung by, said to say good night," Henry said. "They'll be back in the morning."

"Perhaps there are more blessings to come." Liza leaned into Henry. "It's possible for a broken heart to heal stronger, bigger… allow love back in."

"I kept looking at Claud, imagining Chris there with her. Sweetness denied, for all of us," Henry mused. "Wait a minute. What are you getting at?"

Liza shrugged. ""Freddy's a total gem. Claud didn't end up here by accident, and there's been miracles left and right lately."

"Match maker, are ya now?" Henry asked.

"We'll see what the new day brings," Liza said. "I'm ready for bed."

"I'm going to hang out with my boy for a bit." Henry kissed her cheek as she rose.

Jimmy ran his fingers over the unopened envelope, looking at his mother's gentle smile. "Rest well, Mom."

Liza turned on her way out of the room, held Henry's eyes, and smiled. "Remember, Henry…"

"I know, Liza. There's a hole in the bucket."

Nightfall complete, Henry and Jimmy sat in silence, comforted by creaks and groans as the house settled into cooler temperatures, reflecting on the structure that held a lifetime of memories. Jimmy slipped his fingers under the envelope's seal, sliding it open and releasing the letter.

Hey Bro…

Think about you every time I look in the mirror. Ha-ha.

It was the connection he needed to let go. It wasn't about closure. That would never happen. He read the last lines out loud, his father in rapt attention.

Can't wait to whip your butt in a game of Canasta. Rumor is that the war is winding down. I met a girl... bringing her home. Can't wait for you to meet her. Until then, take care of the folks. Shuffle those cards… High five, brother.
Your Other Self
Chris

Jimmy looked at the black sky through the windowpanes, wondering what conspired in the stars and the greater universe to bring all of them to this moment. He turned to Henry's hand on his shoulder.

"Full circle, Dad."

Little Sister Mountain Putucusi glistened under the silver gaze of the moon as mist curled through the crevices of her rocky slopes and wove between the trees, settling over the land like a whisper from the ancient ones, a breath between past and future. The holder of balance and a keeper of harmony, she would remain for all time.

Through the sacred terraces of the stone city, King Llama and Chris moved like spirits at the edge of dream and wakefulness. They paused now and then, heads tilting as if listening to echoes of the past, gathering unseen impressions, fragments of memory and wisdom, to carry forth to the mountain peaks, where they would join ancestors.

Rainbow light trickled through the fabric of dreamtime, drifting like liquid silk into the hearts of all who walked the earth, weaving the seen and unseen, the known and the yet-to-be, binding souls to possibilities beyond imagining.

On a lower terrace, a pregnant llama lay in quiet anticipation, her breath steady, her spirit calm. The birth of twins was near, a sacred doubling, a gift from the unseen realms.

And far to the north, in a pasture in Oregon, Domingo and Bacardi lay with their legs folded underneath them, their long necks stretched toward the stars, silent sentinels of the land. Though miles and lifetimes apart, they heard the whisper of the rainbow dreamtime, felt the rhythm of something greater.

TWENTY-TWO

August 1980

Freddy's Jeep jolted over the old root near the big willow, rattling the gear in the back.

"I met you and the llamas on the same day." A grin spread across Claud's face. "One of the strangest, most wonderful days of my life. They were babies then, and now, what do you think they weigh?"

"Oh, I'd say around three hundred pounds," Freddy said, hopping out of the Jeep. "They'll keep growing for a few more years." With burlap sacks slung over their shoulders, filled with apples and carrots, they strolled into the pasture hand in hand. Sensing a treat, the llamas trotted toward them, soft noses already sniffing the air.

"Remember when they used to either bolt or spit at us?" Freddy chuckled. "Now I swear, they'd climb right into the truck if we let 'em."

"Well, you're pretty convincing," Claud teased. "Even my mother loves you."

Freddy let out a low chuckle. "Yeah, Bakersfield... that was one heck of an introduction. Rosie's alright, though. We're all just shaped by where we come from, you know? Think she'll make it to the wedding?"

"She wouldn't miss it," Claud said. "She called it a miracle that I found a good man to take care of me."

"That's funny, my parents said the same thing about you."

Claud nudged him with a lighthearted poke. "Ever miss San Francisco? Think about going back?"

"Once in a while," Freddy admitted.

"I loved it when we visited. Your folks are a riot."

"A vet in Sonoma offered me a job at his practice last year. Needed someone for the large animals in outlying areas. But I like it here. The clinic's doing great, and when you're not helping Martha deliver babies, I love having you at the office. The staff adore you, but what matters more, so do the animals."

Claud sighed, looking out over the fields. "Never in a million years did I picture this life. I went into the Army and Vietnam, mostly to get away from my mother. Then Chris came along, if only for a minute, but long enough to set all this into motion."

Ankle-high grass tickling their legs, they stood with arms around each other, taking in the quiet of the day. The llamas munched on the dewy grass, their jaws moving slowly, before pausing to lift their heads. Their brown, saucer-like eyes gleamed with curiosity, reflecting the soft light of the late afternoon, as the breeze rustled through the nearby trees. Long, velvet lashes flickered as if they understood that another fresh start was occurring in this ever-spinning world.

"Henry and Liza think we should have our wedding out here in the pasture," he said. "This place has kinda turned into the heart of the community. What do you think?"

Claud's eyes sparkled with excitement, and then, with a burst of joy, she spun in circles, arms flung high toward the sky. "It would be perfect!"

"So that's a yes?" Freddy laughed.

"Oh, yes!" she beamed, eyes sparkling with mischief. "No doubt my mother will have an opinion on my reckless ways, but perhaps for the first time, she'll be able to let go and enjoy the moment."

Freddy grinned. "How about October 7th? Give our folks time to plan their travel, and us about six weeks to pull it together.

"It'll be so much fun! The llamas can be part of the wedding! And Katherine and Jimmy's kids running around... music, laughter, all of it." She swept her arms in a circle, inviting the trees and the abundance of life to partake in their plan. "Let's do it!"

Freddy grabbed her hand. "Liza invited us to dinner. Let's go tell 'em the news."

TWENTY-THREE

October 7, 1980

Jimmy parked the tractor at the crest of the hill. Tall, lush grass swayed, and the quiet embrace of pine and juniper settled in around him like an old friend. He jumped down, giving the fender a pat, its paint worn to a soft matte by years of sun and work.

"You've been a mighty good partner, Harvester."

A wave of wistfulness rose as he reached into the empty space beside him, half expecting to find his twin brother Chris there. His other self, always within reach. The woman Chris had brought into their lives through the long shadow of the Vietnam War was now kin. And today, Claud would marry Freddy.

Porta pots, a tent for the bride, another for the groom, and chairs with an aisle wide enough for llamas. He shook his head and chuckled. Who would have thought it? Llamas? After all they'd been through. Chatter drew his attention to the shelter he and Henry built.

Katherine and Claud stepped out, leading Domingo and Bacardi. Their red leads, woven with gold and silver threads, sparkled in the morning sunlight. Cloaked in handmade quilts of rainbow colors, each llama had chains of daisies, carnations, and yellow roses tipped with crimson draped across their chests, and loose flowers woven into tufts of hair on their necks and crown. He chuckled watching Katherine attempt to secure a top hat on

Domingo, but the llama raised his nose and flattened his ears, a sure sign he'd had enough, and a spit was forthcoming. She tossed the top hat away, and Domingo began to relax but watched her out of the corner of his eye.

Near the bride's tent, Jimmy double-checked the music system. He'd spent days getting music together. Abba for Freddy's parents, Starship for him, and he even got that new song by Leonard Cohen for his parents. Yesterday, they were waltzing around the house like teenagers, "Dance Me to the End of Love" blaring on the record player. He flipped on the switches, expecting the green lights and crackling sounds of speakers to come to life. Nothing.

"Dag gone it."

"What's the matter, hon?" Katherine wandered over.

"No power, no sound." He wiggled the cables, unplugged them, and plugged them back in. "Mom and Dad might have to sing their Hole in the Bucket song."

Katherine giggled. "Now that would be something, eh? An argument song for Freddy and Claud to begin their married life with. They can sing it in German."

"Well, too late to do anything about it." Jimmy shrugged. "Worked fine yesterday."

"Gotta take Claud back to the house to have her hair done. Your mom is getting the twins ready." She looked over at the rope of flowers hanging around Domingo and Bacardi's neck. "Keep an eye on those two, will you? Hopefully they don't eat all the flowers before everyone gets here, eh?"

Jimmy rolled his eyes, but grinned down, bending to kiss her. "Hey, beautiful."

"Not now," Katherine laughed, turning to Claud. "Ready?"

He waved as they drove away and then turned back to the sound system. He replugged all the wires, checked the switches. Not even a crackle. Guests would start arriving soon, and he still needed to get dressed. The sound of Freddy's Jeep bouncing up the hill was a welcome distraction.

"Nervous Freddy?" Jimmy called out.

"Nah." Freddy nodded over at the llamas. "With this magic here? What's the problem?"

"Sound system worked fine yesterday, and now not a peep." Jimmy shrugged.

A young woman stepped out of the Jeep, setting her guitar case on the ground. "Wow, llamas." She walked over to Domingo and Bacardi.

Freddy grinned. "We might have a fallback." They looked over and saw the woman nose to nose with Domingo, giggling. "If she doesn't get spit on that is."

The woman flashed them a grin, eyes warm. "These guys are so cool."

"Kate Wolf is a friend from San Francisco, caught a ride with the folks. She has the voice of an angel and brought her guitar along. Said she has a song rolling around in her head fitting for a wedding. Asked if she could try it out, that is, if we can tear her away from the llamas."

"Kate… good name." Jimmy walked over and shook her hand. "You just missed my wife. Her name is Katherine. Can't have enough Kats around! Makes everything better."

"I look forward to meeting her."

"Where are your folks?" Jimmy asked Freddy.

"They'll be along with the preacher any minute."

Jimmy scratched his head, looking at the dead sound system. "Life's little surprises. Thanks, Kate. Can't wait to hear your new song. Need anything?"

"Got all I need right here," Kate Wolf said, patting her guitar.

"May the good vibes keep coming," Jimmy glanced at his watch. "I need to get back to the house and get dressed. Won't take long."

"My clothes are in the truck," Freddy said. "I'll pop into the tent and change in a bit."

They looked up at the sound of a truck. "Here comes the minister now," Jimmy said. "Got this?"

"Yeah," Freddy looked up as the llamas grew near, a look of expectancy on their faces. "We've got this. Happen to have a bag of apples with me."

"Make sure they don't eat the flowers…" Jimmy's voice faded as the tractor roared to life.

TWENTY-FOUR

Claud, barefoot under a flowing white dress and flowers woven in her hair, fidgeted inside the tent. "What if I have to pee?"

"We'll figure it out." Katherine gave a knowing smile to Liza. "Hi Rosie," Katherine called out, relieved to see Claud's mother come in. "You've got a nervous daughter here."

Rosie took her daughter's hands, looking at her from head to toe.

"What's wrong, Mom? Don't you like my dress? Is it my hair?"

"You're such a beauty." Rosie kissed Claud on the cheek. "Freddy's a lucky man. Barefoot?"

"I like the feel of grass under my feet."

"You've always been a bit of a wild girl. But you turned out all right. You're a nurse, after all."

"Thanks, Mom."

Liza peeked out of the tent, then turned, beaming at the women. "It's time. Here's Henry. And Jimmy's calling you, Katherine."

"Okay! Wish us luck, eh?" Katherine left, looking over her shoulder. "You look marvelous, Mrs. Claud."

"Take good care of my girl," Rosie looked up at Henry, hugging Claud.

"I've got her," Henry said. "Don't you worry about a thing."

Liza took Rosie's arm, guiding her towards the aisle, stopping to greet Christina and Jimmy Jr. as their parents nestled them onto the backs of llamas.

"My, I've never seen a wedding such as this," Rosie said as Liza guided her down the aisle, greeting community members as they passed. "My daughter's barefoot, and everyone has flowers in their hair."

"Festive, isn't it?" Liza asked, stopping at the second row. "Rosie, I'd like you to meet Helen. She's a friend from church."

"Happy to meet you." Rosie took Helen's hand, noticing a slight wrinkle in her brow.

"Everything okay?" Liza asked.

"Oh," Helen said. "Just the usual shenanigans one comes to expect around here."

Liza smiled and winked at Rosie, took her hand and led her to their seats in the front row. She looked up to the sound of a guitar being tuned. Kate Wolf laughed at Max's excitement as he took a harmonica out of his pocket.

Freddy's mother leaned in as he took her arm, guiding her down the aisle. "I can't believe it, Bobo. You even have llamas at your wedding."

"Of course. You raised a son to believe in magic, right?" He escorted her to her front row seat and kissed her cheek. "Thanks for everything, Mom."

"Oh, Bobo." His mom's eyes moistened with tears. "All I ever wanted for you is to be happy."

"I'm happier than I ever thought possible." He gave her one last hug, then joined his father and the minister, who raised a bell, calling the group together.

In the rear, Katherine stood ready, Domingo's braided lead in her hand. Jimmy Jr., festive in his pin-striped suit and top hat with brown curls popping out of the side, held on to his basket of flower petals. "Is it time for the flowers, Mama?"

"No, not yet." Katherine laughed as Jimmy steadied Christina on Bacardi's back, drawing a soft snort from the llama.

"Got this?" Jimmy asked Christina, pinching her cheek. She giggled, picking up a handful of flower petals from the basket perched in front of her, tossing them into the air. The flower petals floated randomly, attached only to the day's magic.

High upon the mountain of Machu Picchu, King Llama sat in quiet majesty, his heart brimming with pride. The Starseeds were a gift from Spirit, luminous threads woven into the tapestry of existence. Their laughter, light and boundless love rippled outward like echoes through time, a healing force shaping the world in unseen ways.

His eyes settled on Freddy, remembering gazing into the young boy's eyes, the raw spark of something greater already rooted in him, like a seed waiting for rain. Now Freddy stood tall and steady, a healer shaped by time and by the quiet truth King Llama had recognized long ago.

Through the eyes of eternity, Chris, now a shimmer of pulsating color, followed Claud's barefooted steps down the aisle towards Freddy. Life was as unpredictable as a summer storm. The morning he died in Vietnam, he had woken with a buzz of excitement, counting down the days until he could bring his bride home. Then, in an instant, a misfired rocket, followed by a deafening blast, everything changed. Yet even in that final moment, joy filled his heart.

And now, standing in this sacred place, Chris felt a knowing deeper than memory. The love that started in that medic's tent so long ago hadn't ended with him. It had stretched beyond one lifetime, flowing forward like a river through time. Unbroken. Eternal.

Freddy's father stepped forward, his grin easy and warm. "Welcome. Nothing makes me prouder than standing here with my son, Freddy, surrounded by friends and family, as we celebrate his union with Claud." He paused, glancing toward Max, who stood nearby, harmonica in hand, deep in whispered conversation with Kate Wolf, tuning her guitar. He chuckled and faced the community. "As luck would have it, the sound system went belly up at the last minute, but it seems the universe had our backs. Our dear friend Kate Wolf, the sweetheart of the San Francisco folk scene, came along from the city and, in the spirt of her generous heart, agreed to sing for us." With one last squeeze of his son's shoulder and an exaggerated bow to the crowd, he sauntered to the front row, settling in beside his wife, a playful twinkle still dancing in his eye.

"Hi, I'm Kate Wolf." She smiled. "Max here has asked to join us with his harmonica. You know how to play that thing, right, Max?"

He grinned, holding the harmonica up to his mouth, played a drawn-out trill, then bowed to the gathering. He paused as his eyes met Helen's and winked at her. Helen's frown softened slightly as a smile slipped from her pursed lips.

Laughter drifted through the group. Kate Wolf smiled and announced, "My new harmonica player, everyone." Sounds of clapping and whistles filled the air.

150

"I've had this song rolling through my head for celebrations just like this," Kate said. "See what you think." She smiled at the crew in the back, who stood ready with the llamas, and began strumming her guitar.

As the first notes rose into the air, a whisper of wind stirred through the ancient city of Machu Picchu, as if the very breath of the mountains had awakened to listen. Melodies of the moment rustled through the trees of Little Sister Mountain Putucusi, where golden light danced upon the leaves like the touch of unseen hands.

King Llama lifted his nose to the sky, his soul attuned to the music as it wove into the fabric of creation. Glowing with the magic of the moment, Chris beheld Claud, clinging to Henry, their spirits bound in the gravity of the moment. So beautiful. He stood in silent awe as a voice, that of an angel, sang out…

"Kind friends all gathered 'round,
there's something I would say:
That what brings us together here
has blessed us all today.
Love has made a circle that holds us all inside.
Where strangers are as family,
loneliness can't hide." [1]

Jimmy Jr. giggled, tossing handfuls of flower petals into the air as Katherine led Domingo, his head held high, down the aisle. Jimmy followed with Bacardi, Christina scooping up handfuls of flowers and flinging them skyward. Soft murmurs and laughter rippled through the crowd as a cascade of colors fell around them.

Bacardi, mid-chomp on a drifting petal, looked shocked as he bumped into Domingo, who had stopped to nibble the flowers woven into Katherine's hair. Laughing, she ducked away, the moment as wild and free as the day itself.

---

[1] Wolf, Kate. Give Yourself to Love. 1983

Liza smiled at Helen's frown. "Oh, that Domingo," she said. "He likes to eat hair." She looked past the llamas and saw Henry wink, a broad grin on his face.

"Well look at that," Kate Wolf said, strumming chords. "You guys are stealing the show. Serenade them up the aisle, won't you, Max?"

And just like that, amidst the sounds of a guitar strumming and harmonica trills, the last flower petals were scattered to the wind. Baskets empty, Katherine and Jimmy guided the llamas off to the side, the whole scene humming with an easy, barefoot kind of joy.

Freddy's breath caught as Claud stepped forward, arm in arm with Henry. Her face tight with nerves, she glanced up and met Freddy's smile. It was like a spark, and with it, a wave of calm washed over her. Her shoulders relaxed, her steps growing steadier as she continued forward, Henry's hand gently clasping hers.

"Let's start again," Kate said. "Everyone sing along this time. Ready Max?"

> *"Kind friends all gathered 'round,*
> *there's something I would say:*
> *That what brings us together here*
> *has blessed us all today.*
> *Love has made a circle that holds us all inside.*
> *Where strangers are as family,*
> *and loneliness can't hide."*

"Beautiful… Now, here's the chorus."

> *"You must give yourself to love,*
> *if love is what you're after.*
> *Open up your hearts to the tears and laughter.*
> *And give yourself to love, give yourself to love."*

Claud felt the soft petals under her feet, the scent of roses drifting up with each step, soothing her nerves. She smiled at Henry, who squeezed her hand. Nearing the front, her heart filled with the joy in her mother's eyes. As she passed, she squeezed her mother's hand, then turned to Freddy, her face soft with love as his eyes silently invited her closer.

"I've walked these mountains in the rain and learned
to love the wind.
I've been up before the sunrise,
to watch the day begin.
I always knew I'd find you,
though I never did know how.
Like sunshine on a cloudy day,
you stand before me now."

"So give yourself to love,
if love is what you're after.
Open up your hearts to, the tears and laughter.
And give yourself to love, give yourself to love."

The air shimmered as a lone guitar strummed, joined by the plaintive cry of Max's harmonica, their melodies weaving through the terraces of Machu Picchu like ancient prayers. Freddy and Claud stood, hands entwined and hearts wide open, as they spoke their vows. Wedding bands slipped onto their fingers and a breath full of joy, they turned, grinning, to face their friends and family as the minister declared them husband and wife. Hand in hand, they strolled down the aisle, wrapped in a wave of cheers, laughter and just a touch of magic.

Golden energy shimmered in the air around them, and as they walked, they were gently reminded of their purpose by the words of the mistress of songs:

"Give yourself to love, if love is what you're after.
Open up your hearts to the tears and laughter, and,
Give yourself to love, give yourself to love..."

Chris, his form a cascade of iridescent light, moved with the music like a spirit born of sound and sky, his presence a radiant pulse of joy woven into the celebration. King Llama gazed across the sacred city, joining hearts with Little Sister Mountain Putucusi, feeling the rhythm of the world shifting around him.

The mountains watched. The stars listened. And love, unyielding and infinite, endured.

EPILOGUE

September 1982

Gentle rain blanketed the mountain range of Machu Picchu during the night, weaving a dream of water and stone. At dawn, a blanket of white mist whispered through the mountains, teased by occasional wisps of green trees and blue sky. As sunlight warmed the day, a rainbow formed from the top of Machu Picchu extending to the ancient Incan city.

Among the mountain peaks, Chris gazed at the stars and galaxies, enchanted by the endless cosmos. No matter how far he ventured, he was always drawn back to Little Sister Mountain Putucusi and the ancient stone city, where nature thrived in every leaf, stone, and breeze, where the past and future wove together in a single eternal thread. And so, on this day, he stood once more upon the sunlit plaza, side by side with King Llama, watching life's unfolding.

On terraces below, birthing sounds filled the air as a pregnant llama, heavy with the weight of new life, gave her final push, and into the world tumbled twin crias, rare in the world of llamas. Their first cries, pure and strong, were carried by the breeze through the stone corridors of the city, up to the peaks where the spirits listened, welcoming the new guardians of the llama nation.

King Llama lowered his head, a knowing glimmer in his eyes. From his first breath as a newborn cria, lifetimes ago, to this moment, where new souls took their first steps upon sacred ground, the circle was complete. He had walked the path of guardian, guiding seekers who journeyed to these ancient mountains, witnessing love and destiny woven thread by thread across the tapestry of time.

His heart swelled with joy as the sound of children's laughter echoed from the faraway pasture in Oregon, echoed on the wind like a song of homecoming. Love endured. Life continued. And as the newborn twins found their legs beneath the golden sun, King Llama turned his gaze toward the peaks, where the wind whispered stories of all that had been and all that was still yet to come.

The late afternoon sun poured down on the Oregon pasture and warm, golden streaks caught the wild curls and bobbing heads of children dancing in a circle.

"Ring around the Rosie, pockets full of Posie, ashes, ashes, all fall down."

Bursting with giggles, they tumbled into the grass. Not far off, Domingo and Bacardi dipped their muzzles into a scratchy burlap sack of grain. They looked up in eager anticipation as Christina and Jimmy Jr. skipped through the grass with a basket of carrots, green leafy tops hanging over the edge.

Nearby, sounds of champagne glasses clinked in toasts of celebration mixed with the hum of conversation. At the center of a long, homespun table sat a weathered, leatherbound book, its worn pages full of stories, love, and a half-century of living. It lay open, a bold declaration etched across the parchment:

"HAPPY 50TH ANNIVERSARY, HENRY AND LIZA."

"No jump!" Claud laughed, pulling her dog to a stop. Claud's belly, round with new life, hardly slowed her down, though the pup's playful antics made every step a bit of a dance. With haunches wiggling and tail wagging, the dog stood poised, waiting for the next move, or maybe just a treat.

Freddy dropped to his knees and wrapped the pup in a hug. Treats forgotten, she smothered his face in happy, slobbery kisses.

"Spoiled rotten," Claud laughed. "But what can we do? She's family."

From across the field, a burst of static crackled through weathered speakers, followed by a sharp whistle that sliced through the warm evening air. Jimmy clambered onto the bed of the pickup. "Alright folks, time to circle up and dance," he called. "Happy Anniversary, Mom and Pops! This one's for you."

Helen looked up at Max's outstretched hand. A softness she had long thought forbidden filled her heart as she took it. The rough callouses on his hand from working the pumps reminded her that he was very much a real human. Joining with the community circle, "Dance Me to the End of Love" filled the air.

"La la, la, la, la la la…"

"Henry led Liza to the heart of the circle and began to dance. Friends danced around them like a living breath, feet lifting in time with the music. Oboes, violins and clarinets blended in a polka rhythm as Leonard Cohen's husky voice filled the air.

Eyes locked in radiant joy as their feet twirled in the grassy pasture, Henry and Liza celebrated life lived on this land, those who came before, and those who would inherit the future. The sun sank into the towering pines, casting long golden shadows over the pasture. Mist rose from the earth like a whispered prayer, curling through the branches and settling over the land, a soft, familiar embrace.

Dancing in sweeping circles, Liza's scarf slipped down, freeing her long, silver hair to cascade around her shoulders. With each turn, the world softened, the evening fog thickening and swirling, wrapping around them like a living being. Shapes blurred, faces faded. Soon you could only feel the person beside you, moving as one, caught in a rhythm deeper than words.

Leonard's voice drifted through the hush and then, like a dream, the fog shifted and stretched into the trees, fading away into the night. And in the soft, misty glow of twilight, Liza danced alone.

King Llama stood upon the upper ridge, his silhouette etched against the boundless sky, a silent watcher as Chris and his father reunited beneath the timeless embrace of Little Sister Mountain Putucusi. Here in this place where the veil between worlds was but a breath, the rhythm of life echoed in the stones, the heartbeat of life always held in the earth we walk on and the heavens which grace our every step. As light danced and time stood still, King Llama bowed his head, honoring the reunion, the love that endured beyond the boundaries of life and death. For in the embrace of the earth and the grace of the heavens, nothing was ever truly lost, only transformed, only remembered, always held.

Five years later...

On the anniversary of Henry's passing, the community gathered once more in the Oregon pasture, a place made sacred by the footsteps of those who had danced, worked, and loved upon its soil, and blessed by the winged ones gliding high above.

Taller now, Jimmy Jr. and Christina moved with ease through the familiar rhythm of setting up tables and chairs, their hands sure and practiced from years spent under this same sun, in this same

158

place. The air held echoes of childhood laughter and old music drifting from past celebrations. Not far off, Domingo and Bacardi stood watch, their curious eyes following every movement, just as they had since the beginning. And like old times, their dad, Jimmy, was locked in a battle with the sound system.

On the table, the same weathered book of life flipped to another chapter as folks swayed to the familiar hum of "Dance Me to the End of Time," the Leonard Cohen song that always brought them back together.

Hands reached for hands, and before long, they were in the familiar circle, dancing, moving in rhythm with the wheel of life, turning ever onward. Jimmy took his mother's hand and led her to the heart of their gathering, where the music and laughter swirled like the wind. They moved together, light on their feet, each skip and twirl widening the circle, their steps tracing the rhythm of the ancient and true.

Liza's eyes swept across the faces of her people, soaking in love, life, and the beauty of it all. They danced beyond the edges of the circle, where the late afternoon mist thickened into the familiar rolling fog, soft, shifting and changing, as everything in this world does.

She met Jimmy's eyes one last time, her smile full of knowing. And then, like a whisper in the wind, Liza faded into the trees as the fog lifted, carried away with the evening.

Katherine stepped forward, slid her hand into Jimmy's, and without a word, the music played on, and the dance continued.

Wrapped in a cloak of time-worn threads, King Llama, Chris, Henry and Liza stood nestled within the folds of Little Sister Mountain Putucusi. Before them, life unfolded in quiet rhythm, each footstep stirring the earth like a heartbeat. Wind whispered through the peaks, carrying echoes of the ancients, the drumbeats of all who had come before, their stories woven into the breath of the mountains.

Far across the expanse of earth and sky, in a sun-kissed Oregon pasture, Katherine and Jimmy, unwilling to let the day slip into memory, swayed together in the golden twilight. The melody of their laughter mingled with the evening breeze as they danced, bare feet pressing into the earth, grounding them in all that had been and all that was to come. At the edge of the pasture, Domingo and Bacardi sat like ancient souls, black-and-white forms, still and wise, watching over their world with the timeless patience of the earth itself.

Above them, a double rainbow unfurled across the heavens, stretching from the sacred peaks of Machu Picchu to the whispering fields of Oregon. Its colors shimmered like strands of woven light, linking past to future, the visible to the unseen, the circle complete.

THE END

AUTHOR NOTES

Several years ago, fresh from a trip to Peru, where Llamas and Alpacas graced nearly every turn, I stumbled upon an ad in my Facebook Buying Club: *Two llamas for dog food. You butcher and haul.*

I didn't hesitate. I picked up the phone and said: "I'll take them." Deep in my bones I knew these llamas had more life to live. They were eighteen years old, and me, a tender sixty-three. We could grow old together. I trusted my husband would (eventually) come around. (He did.) The years that followed were filled with unexpected adventures, and stories to be told.

Domingo passed in 2018 at age twenty-five. Bacardi, his loyal companion from birth, stayed with us until 2022, living to the age of 28, matching the oldest documented llama on record, before passing of natural causes. The prologue of this book comes from the night of his death and the quiet vigil we held by his side.

During the early days of the pandemic, I came across a Facebook post by Fredy, a Peruvian *Paqo*, Porter, and Guide. In the photo, he knelt in reverence before a white llama on Machu Picchu. With tourism shuttered, it was a time of hardship in Peru. He had gone to check on the animals. Beneath the image, he wrote:

King Llama says all will be well.

I replied with a picture of Bacardi, who looked like a twin to the llama in his photo, bridging a moment across time, continents, and spirit. And thus, *Starseeds* was born.

Starseeds is a journey of hope, healing, and love. In that spirit, I want to honor the legacy of folk singer Kate Wolf, whose music captures the heart of everything this story aspires to share. Her songs echo with honesty, compassion, and grace, qualities that deeply informed the message of this book. I am especially grateful to the Wolf family for allowing me to include the lyrics to her song, *Give Yourself to Love*, in my story.

If you haven't yet discovered her music, I encourage you to listen. Check out www.KateWolf.com to learn more about Kate Wolf, her life and legacy.

ACKNOWLEDGEMENTS

Thea Constantine: From our early days of writing at Beaterville Café, you always make writing fun, inspirational and honest.

Christi Krug: From Wildfire Writing to 18 years of mentorship, your ability to see the positive and inspire, peppered with honest critique, is priceless.

Fellow writers, Beta Readers and Critique Group: You took me in, listened to my stories and shared yours with me. Thank you for believing in me. I return that belief in you wholeheartedly. Special thanks to

Joanna Wiley and GC Troop for insights and edits.

Larry – my husband, best friend, historian and fellow journeyer. It's been an adventure, hasn't it? Charley and Phillip – my sons. Thank you for walking this life with me and teaching me to be a better human.

A heart full of gratitude to my Peruvian family, all whose paths crossed with mine, every moment an experience in healing, love and grace.

Emily Papel – Editor: You understand my writing and meet me where I am. Forever grateful.

Get Covers.com – My first time with you for cover design. Won't be the last! Thank you.

Finally, to all the animals that surround me every day, convincing me that all will be better if I just step outside for a moment and walk barefoot in the grass.

You can find me at:
Facebook: Sue Paterson – writer
Website: suepatersonauthor.com

In the algorithms of life, especially on Amazon and other sites for books, reviews are everything.
If you have gotten this far, please consider writing a review.
Thank you.

www.ingramcontent.com/pod-product-compliance
Lightning Source LLC
Chambersburg PA
CBHW032311310726

48973CB00008B/2604